DOG HOUSE

A Story About Domestic Violence, Hope, And Survival

TERRI BRITT WATTS

ISBN: 978-1-7370998-2-6

TABLE OF CONTENTS

ACKNOWLEDGEMENTS

I must acknowledge my Savior, Jesus Christ because He is the one who has given me this gift of writing. I share the joy of sharing my stories with you. If you don't have a relationship with the Lord, you need one. Accept Him as your personal Savior.

If you don't understand what I'm saying, pick up your Bible and begin reading any of the four Gospels - Matthew, Mark, Luke, and John. In these four books, you will discover something powerful. The Gospels show how much the Father loves us despite our wicked ways. The beauty of God's message to us is we don't have to die and go to Hell. God provided a way for us to be with Him in Heaven for eternity. Which route will you choose? I am going to Heaven, what about you?

Take time out today to accept the gift God has presented before you. His Son, Jesus Christ, is the best gift ever! Go to a quiet place or call a saved friend to guide you. With all sincerity, confess you are a sinner to the Lord. Ask for forgiveness, and then ask Jesus to come into your heart today. Guess what? He will do it! Afterward, find a good church that teaches God's word and get baptized. Baptism is a public showing of your faith.

A Prayer of Repentance and Acceptance of Salvation and Eternal Life Through Jesus Christ

Dear Lord, I am a sinner. I repent for every sin I've ever committed against you. I am sorry for the wrongs I've done. I know that you are God and that you gave your only begotten Son, Jesus, to die for my sins so that I may have eternal life with you. I believe

Jesus died for me, and I believe He rose from the dead. Thank you, Jesus, for taking my place on the cross. I believe that you are the Son of the Living God. Please come into my heart, Jesus. I accept you as my Lord and Savior! Thank you, Jesus, for saving my soul.
IN JESUS' NAME, AMEN.

If you have not yet had this discussion with God, you need to. It doesn't matter how nice a person you think you are. It doesn't matter who you are, your financial status, or whatever. If you have not received Christ as your personal Savior, you cannot live eternally with the Lord.

After you say this prayer, you will be a work in progress, just like me, and other children of God. Know that you will have peace and joy that surpasses all understanding. It doesn't mean you won't have troubles, because you will. However, we who are children of God, can take all of our burdens to Him, and leave them there! He will lead and guide us.

To Our Children

Rickey Caldwell
Timothy Caldwell
David Watts Jr.
Chantel Watts
You are a blessing to us! Live wise, accept wisdom,
cherish God's word and live an abundant life.

To Our Grandchildren

Malachi
Mataya
Naomi
Lexington
Sumerlin
Oliver
Kendall
Kameron

Oh, how we thank God for you! We love you and will continue to love you until the Lord calls us home. You have brought great joy into our lives. Listen to your parents, for they have great wisdom to share. Find the Lord, keep His Word close to you, and He will keep His promises for you.

NOTES

Doghouse is a story based on true events. Some places, names, and actual events have been changed so as not to cause disturbances of any type or to any person.

Living As If You Are the Problem

Did you know that the term wife-beating stood legal in the United States until 1920? Wife beating is the same as domestic violence. It is just written or stated as such for the era of that time, the 1920s. In 1970, the women's rights movement became prevalent and launched modern attention to domestic violence.

These movements sparked national concern about women being beaten by their husbands. These movements may have slowed the frequency of domestic violence reports. However, there is certainly concern that the situation is rising again.

According to Time Magazine, women and children are not any safer now than before the movements. It has been found that most women die from gunshot wounds more than any other method of killing by their spouse, boyfriend, or partner.

Men are not the only abusers. Sometimes women abuse their husbands, boyfriends, or partners. Often, your live-in adult child may be the abuser. Nonetheless, and whoever the abuser is, please know that there is help. We must recognize the signs and learn how to escape.

As a domestic violence survivor, I'm here to share my story. There is hope. You don't deserve violent treatment in a manner that causes harm to your physical or mental state. You did not cause your abuser to act abusively. That is who they are. Upon reading this book, and realizing that you are in an abusive relationship, seek help. There is help! I will share that and more as you delve into this book.

My Christian sisters and brothers, please know that the Lord loves you. He does! Yes, He hates divorce, but He calls you to live in peace. I will expound more on that later. Do not live with ANYONE who calls you out of your name, shoves, pushes, or controls your coming and goings. Trust me, those unwanted behaviors will continue.

The behaviors listed above are more subtle than others. Oh, yes, many abusive behaviors are so elusive that you will feel like it's nothing. Pay attention because it is definitely something. It will grow until it reaches its full capacity. When it does, it will explode, causing bodily harm, mental depletion, or death.

From my experiences, research, and God's word, we will unpack this evil called domestic violence. We will learn the simplicity of shrewd red flags, patterns, the severity of warnings, when to walk, when to run, who to call, and when not to look back.

God said in His word. I know the plans I have for you. They are plans for good and not for disaster, to give you a future and a hope." (Jeremiah 29:11). This scripture tells me that God our Father did not create me for disaster, but He has a future for me along with hope. We are going to get deep into this story, my story. I hope you're ready.

CHAPTER I

It is the early 1970s, and Laura Clayton finds herself in peril. The loving hands she trusted 13 years ago are gone. Her once statuesque spouse replaces love with brutal attacks. Will she survive? Laura is definitely doused with tenacity, grit, and spunk. However, one must wonder if she is strong enough to salvage her future?

Laura Clayton ran as fast as she could through the thicket brush. Thorns pierced her legs, arms, and hands as she struggled to get away from her obtrusive abuser. At a glance, she recognized a spot in the woods where she could hide and be safe – at least for a little while. It was cold, damp, and dreary on that Tuesday evening. Laura trembled from the brisk breeze – drawing her attention away from her assailant.

Perry, a stout, husky man, chased his prey with no remorse. "Laura!" he shouted while frantically glancing around. Laura nestled tightly into her hiding place, trying hard not to breathe. She shivered from the cold. Perry's steps grew louder amid the crumbling leaves. "Laura, you better get your tail back here! Come on Sweetheart. You know I didn't mean it." Perry sighed, "It's all your fault – you have to stop making me so mad."

Perry lightened his step in hopes of wooing Laura from her safe place. He stopped, glanced around, and spotted something white among the brush. He wooed again.

"Laura, Baby, I'm sorry – how many times do you want me to say it – huh? I'm sorry!" Perry took a side path to reach Laura. She frantically glanced around while shaking.

"Ugghh!" She screamed as Perry yanked her up by her thick bushy hair. His unintentional apologies proved debauched, at least on the way back to the house. Laura stumbled as Perry dragged her back toward home. "Perry please take the walking path; I'm already cut up from the bristles."

"You should have thought about that when you decided to run away – and to run away from me – what were you thinking? What would my co-workers think if they found out you left me – huh?" Perry jerked Laura by the hair and pulled her up to face him. He clenched his teeth with a seething desire to hit her. "I am so sick and tired of you playing these silly games, Laura. If you would do what the hell I ask you to do, we wouldn't be out here traipsing around in these freaking woods, like some stupid animals!"

Perry lifted his hand, and Laura winced quickly and turned away from Perry. He gently grazed his hand over her hair and then to the side of her face. He looked around precariously, licked his lips, and then forced Laura to the ground.

"Oh, Perry, no, please don't," she whimpered.

Perry hurriedly unzipped his pants, snatched Laura's nightgown out of the way, and climbed on top of her. She bit her bottom lip while tears streamed from her eyes. To make time pass – Laura stared at the half-moon and tried to count the stars. She wondered what her mom and dad were doing and if the kids were OK. She grimaced at Perry's thrusts and tried to refocus on something new, anything until he finished raping her. Soon the old familiar grunts and groans alerted her it was over.

At that point, Laura didn't care anymore. That was her life – her story, one she wished she could erase and rewrite. Laura continued to lie in the woods – watching Perry stagger toward their home. She managed to pick herself up off the ground. Blood from the scratches and pierces from thorns seeped through her gown. *Lord, I need to get away from this man before he kills me. Please give me the strength to leave. I cannot keep going on like this!"* She wept as she walked home.

Laura crept into the back door. She could hear the shower water running in the master bath and hurriedly made her way to the guest bathroom to shower. Quickly she locked the door behind her. Sometimes she was safe behind locked doors, and then sometimes, she was not. At this point, Laura just wanted to wash away the shame that consumed her body. *No soap*, she reminded herself. Laura looked down at the many scratches on her legs and arms. She wept again. *Lord, I need you – can't take this too much longer. Why don't you just take me! I'm so tired of this life, Jesus – just please, please take me!"*

Laura stood 5'3" – a bit chunky for her height. Her once mocha smooth skin glowed each time she showered. But not this time. It stood ripped with lines imitating a scatter plot graph. Her hair was so beautiful that she could wear it straight or curly.

Her hairdresser used to always tell her, "Girl, women would die to have your hair." Laura smiled while staring into the mirror, thinking about Vanessa, her hairdresser, and her comments. As she ran her fingers through her hair, she noticed blood on the tips of her fingers. Laura examined the area again and felt a lock of hair missing. Instantly, she remembered Perry snatching her up from the ground by her hair after he found her. *"That bastard!"* Shaking her head frantically from side to side, she murmured, *"I have to get out of here; that is all there is to it. I can't stay here."*

"Where are you going, Mommy?" Lisa asked. Abruptly, Laura whirled around to find Lisa, her nine-year-old daughter standing in the doorway and wiping sleep from her eyes. Choking back tears, and thankful she had put on her robe before Lisa's entrance, Laura ran over to clutch Lisa into her arms.

"Oh, sweetheart, Mommy was just thinking about taking a little trip."

"Oh, goody, can I go too! Wait a minute, what kind of trip – and how long are we going to be gone?"

"Does it matter? Just as long as we have fun?"

"Is Daddy coming?"

Laura cringed at the sound of Lisa's innocent inquiry. "No, Baby, he may have to work… anyway, why are you up so late?"

"I had to use the bathroom?"

"Sweetie, um, you have a bathroom next to your room, why didn't you use that one?"

Lisa wiped her eyes again and looked at her mom, "I thought I heard you crying so I wanted to check on you."

Laura stooped down, nuzzled her face on Lisa's cheek, and patted Lisa on her back.

"Don't you worry about me; I will be just fine. Go use the bathroom. I want you to get some rest before school tomorrow."

Laura gently guided Lisa toward the bathroom and closed the door behind her.

Afterward, she called the school's office and left a message. She would not be working on Wednesday. Laura crept into the guest bedroom, locked the door, climbed into bed, and slept until noon.

———————

On Thursday morning, Laura managed to drag herself out of bed to face yet another consortium on why she was not at work again for the fourth time that month.

"So, what is the issue this time, Laura – Lisa got a cold, or Gregory having some sort of a tantrum?" Vivian, Laura's co-worker snorted.

"You leave my babies out of this. It's none of your business why I am absent. I don't have to answer to you, heifer!"

"Oh my, aren't we testy today–and after a day off from work!" Vivian taunted.

Laura jumped from her chair. "I'm warning you, keep out of my business, or you may need several days off after I'm done with you!"

"Sit down Laura," Amelia said as she comforted Laura with soft caresses to her back. "You don't have to answer to her anyway." Amelia then stared at Vivian with a long gaze.

"Good morning ladies, I'm glad you all could make it today. Ah, it is such a beautiful morning out, don't you all agree?" Cassandra placed her belongings into her desk drawer and sat to begin the meeting.

"You all know why we are here. Now I've made it known that I respect families and the issues that it brings. But what I don't like is for you to take advantage of my kindness and call out of work at will. It is so hard to get reputable substitute teachers to take your place, especially when you do not leave a pertinent lesson plan."

Cassandra then cast her gaze toward Laura and continued. "If there are some sort of problems that you are going through, you can wait until after the meeting to talk with me or we can discuss any matter after school. But ladies, I need you at work every day unless you are laid up at the hospital, or something is seriously wrong with your child. Any questions?" The principal began pulling sticky notes down from her computer and prioritizing them for that day's duties. Occasionally, she would glance to see if anyone had anything to say – and then she would go back to organizing her desk for Thursday's tasks.

"No questions?" Cassandra reiterated.

Some mumbled as they got up from the table and moseyed to their morning duties and or classrooms. However, Laura lagged, standing while muddling through papers, notes, and vanilla folders. Cassandra glanced, once again, to see some depart her office – all but Laura. She stopped what she was doing, folded her hands in front of her, and then gestured for Laura to sit back down.

Laura sat and said, "You know what, Mrs. Pullman, I think I'll talk to you after school, if that's OK with you," Laura then put her head down after her statement.

"Laura, what is it – this is not like you to call out every week. Are the children ok? Are things ok with your folks? I mean, I'm not understanding the truancies."

Again, Laura lowered her head. "I promise I'll stop by after school and talk with you, OK?"

Sighing, Cassandra nodded.

CHAPTER II

Laura drove the agonizing drive home from work. Thoughts of Perry's constant abuse absorbed her mind. She realized she must seek help, or her life could end, and end abruptly. If this tragedy were to take place, it would kill her parents.

During her childhood, she witnessed her dad's abusive behavior toward her mom. She never understood why her mother stayed. Nancy, her mother, had no job. Laura's dad stood to be the family's main support. Nancy, in retrospect, had no place else she could turn. If she did leave, how was she to provide for Laura and her four siblings?

The abuse lasted for years until Nancy ended up in the hospital fighting for her life. Laura's grandparents, staunch Christians, constantly spoke to their son, Paul, about how he treated his wife, Nancy. Their words fell on death's ears. There was a curse – a curse in the Maxwell's family line that had not been broken. And until it is broken, the abuse would continue to trickle down from generation to generation. Acceptance of abuse will undoubtedly become the norm.

Not only does the curse persist from lineage to lineage but it tends to spill over into relationships, in that it is almost accepted behavior. Laura's mother endured it for years, so she, Laura, was taking on a demon from her past and who knows how far back in their family line of women who have endured, condoned, and lived through such ill-treatment?

Laura finally reached her ranch-style home. As the garage door rose, she saw Perry's car. *"What in the heck is he doing home from work so early!"* she thought. Nervously, she gathered her briefcase and went inside. As she entered the kitchen, she saw a bouquet of roses on the counter and the aroma of simmering spaghetti with toasted garlic bread in the oven. The table was set for four. A crisp salad, topped with all of Laura's favorites centered the table.

"Hi Laura," Perry appeared while sheepishly donning an apron. He walked over to the stove and turned it off. He then took the garlic bread from the oven.

Laura slowly took her gaze off the table and looked at Perry. Flashbacks of Tuesday night kept impeding her mind. She made a quick step toward the bedroom, but Perry grabbed her by the arm. Never looking up at Perry, she stopped dead in her tracks, hoping not to anger him.

"Laura," he spoke gently, "I did this for you. I know I have been so terrible this past month, and I want to make it up to you. Please, will you allow me to do that?"

Laura stood still, not acknowledging Perry with her eyes. Finally, she spoke.

"Where are Lisa and Greg?"

Perry could feel her trembling and released his grip from her arm. As soon as he did, she fled to their rooms and found them quietly doing their homework. As her presence alerted them, they jumped from their seats and greeted her cheerfully.

"Mom, you're home," they chimed in unison.

Lisa interjected, "Dad is cooking spaghetti and garlic bread, my favorite," she beamed while rubbing her tummy.

Laura smiled. The children's gleeful disposition lifted her spirits. The tension she felt earlier, soon left her and she allowed the peaceful transformation to take its place. Perry slowly entered the union. Laura half-heartedly acknowledged his presence, smiled, and looked at the children as she spoke.

"Yep, it does smell good, I have to agree to that."

"Yes it does," Greg added, "and I can't wait until we can eat!"

"Well, it's ready," said Perry.

"Yay!" exclaimed the children. "We are starving!" They hurriedly brushed passed their parents and ran toward the kitchen.

"Go wash your hands first," demanded Perry.

"Yes Sir!"

Soon, the Claytons sat to pander in their meal. Laura sat quietly as she forced bite after bite. Perry glanced at his wife between bites and finally asked.

"Is it not to your liking, Laura?"

"Oh, no, it is delicious," she said while wiping her mouth. "I'm not that… "

"… you're not that hungry," Perry interrupted, finishing Laura's sentence.

"No, no, I am hungry – it's just that my stomach has been bothering me lately."

Gregory scoffed down his portion and asked for more. "It is soooo good to me. Daddy, you must make this more often. I could eat spaghetti every day!"

"It is good, but I don't want to eat it every day," Lisa blared.

"Girl, shut up! I said, Daddy could cook spaghetti every day, because that is what I want!" Greg then poked himself in the chest and passed his plate to be refilled.

Perry chuckled, and then remarked, "Boy you are something else."

Lisa spoke with a roll of her eyes, "Rude is what he is – just plain ole rude."

Greg performed a pretentious stance to startle Lisa. She rolled her eyes again, never flinching.

"Alright, you two, enough," Laura interjected. "Finish your dinner so you can return to your homework."

After the children had their fill of Perry's palatable meal, they collected their used dishes, rinsed them off, and placed them into the dishwasher. Both returned to their rooms bickering about anything that would satisfy their emotions at that moment. Laura stood to clear her plate.

"Laura, please could you sit for a moment – we need to talk. I've tried and tried to figure out how I can make this right. I hate when those flare-ups occur. I don't like being like this. I don't like the feelings that come over me–and all at once."

Laura then looked to face her husband of 13 years. His husky build is what drew her to him. She met him at a friend's house during the spring. There he stood, just a little taller than she. His stature was maybe 5'10. Perry lifted heavyweights in those days which attributed to his husky physique. His vanilla complexion and honey brown eyes added to his attributes. Instantly, Laura fell head-over-heels in love with Perry. Now she's questioning her fall.

"So, instead you empty your emotions onto me, is that right, Perry? You used me, to make you feel better. You used me as your punching bag to release all your unwanted fears – is that right, Perry?"

At her remark, Perry bit his bottom lip to suppress his anger. "You have every right to be mad at me – you do. But I'm trying here." He then looked at Laura. "I love you. I do, Laura. And I know these past few months have been hell for you. They have served me the same way."

"How so, Perry?" Laura sarcastically questioned as she placed her hand on her hip. "Please enlighten me because the last time I checked, you weren't the one forced to do something you did not want to do! The last time I checked, you were not used as a punching bag! So, please tell me how in the hell can you say your feelings resemble mine?"

"No, no," Perry sighs with a shake of his head and tries to find a way to express his feelings. "What I mean, Laura is that after I do what I do to you, it makes me feel ill – I don't know. It is hard to explain. I guess you can say I do have a conscience. I want to stop, but I don't know how." Perry then got out of his chair and took a couple of steps toward Laura. She cautiously positioned herself to rise.

"Do you think this meal is going to mend the many tears in my heart? Do ya – do you actually believe that we are good to go now, Perry? I have seen this movie play so many times that I can recite every line and am well aware of what's going to happen before it does. But here, lately, you are changing the script. Oh, I would have been ready for you Tuesday, but you caught me in my sleep. I would have been dressed, and ready to flee. You are getting crafty with your manipulation and I'm sick of it! I'd rather die than keep living this way!"

"Laura, please don't say that," pleaded Perry. "I told you I was sorry; what more do you want me to do. You know you have a part in this too."

"O-kay, that's my cue." Laura shoved her plate of uneaten meal across the table and moved to exit the dining area. Perry reached for her out of pretense, but she evaded his grasp. Laura then dashed to the kitchen and armed herself with a kitchen knife.

"Come any closer and you will lose your dinner on this very day," she screeched while stomping her foot.

Perry put his hands in the air, profiling a smirk. "You wouldn't do that. You don't have it in you." He stepped closer.

"I mean it, Perry," Laura screamed with a quivering voice. "I'll do it – don't come any closer!" Perry still standing with hands raised, seemed to enjoy the perilous strain Laura was experiencing.

"Alright, alright," Perry said while lowering his hands and stepping backward. Laura, still armed, hurriedly walked past Perry. "Narcissistic bastard," she whispered, as she went toward the children's bedrooms which were side by side, she witnessed their stance on the threshold of their bedrooms. Quickly, she discretely placed the knife beside the right side of her thigh as she walked past.

"Mom, what are you guys fighting about now?" asked Greg. "We just had some good food and y'all are fighting again?"

Laura, murmured, "Go finish your homework." She then walked into the guest bedroom, closed the door, and locked it.

Laura lay on the bed and stared at the ceiling. Now and then she would jump at the sound of Perry's footsteps. She reminisced on how she met Perry and how their relationship evolved. Perry didn't seem to have a mean bone in his body. He was a great provider and boy could he cook. Their relationship seemed to make them inseparable. What happened to them? What caused Perry to change so directly? She thought about what Perry said on Tuesday… "You know this is your fault too." *But how could it be my fault?* she thought.

Laura began to examine every aspect of her life with Perry. What in the world had she done to have her husband turn against her as he has? Of course, and after the children were born, she had put on a little weight, but who hadn't after giving birth? Perry had never mentioned her weight. At 5'3" Laura was now 200 lbs. Throughout their marriage, she had noticed Perry's compliments of her once slim build had since faded. He didn't look at her the same as he used to. But even before the children were born, she noticed little antics here and there. The name-calling, embarrassing and awkward situations around family and friends.

She remembered one hot sunny day; she and Perry went to get ice cream. They were so happy that day. It was the first time, Perry met her mother, Nancy. On this particular day, Laura desired a banana split. So off to the ice-cream polar they go. Perry drove his car, a metallic blue, two-door Monte Carlo. Perry has always relished his cars. Sometimes, Laura would tease him intimately, and say, "I wish you rubbed on me as much as you rub on that car!" Perry ignored her nifty remark and would continue detailing his prize possession.

Once the choices of ice cream had been made, the three started back home, licking the drippings so as not to make a mess in Perry's car. Soon they arrived home and as Nancy, who sat in the front, got out and reached for the seat to pull it forward, Laura pushed the seat forward as well. The mechanics of the movement caused Laura to drop her banana split on the back seat of the car. Laura screeched at the accident. "Oh no, Perry! I am so sorry. I just dropped my entire ice cream container on the seat. Would you grab some paper towels so I can get it up? Laura vividly remembered Perry's reaction. He abruptly peered down toward the back seat.

"You did what?" he screamed.

Laura, surprised at his response, looked up at him to see if he was angry, concerned about her lost ice cream, or wondered if she cut his leather car seats with a box knife.

"I'm so sorry, yeah, I dropped my ice cream as I tried to help Mom push the seat up so that I could get out. If you get me a few paper towels I can get it up quickly."

"I can't believe you dropped that freaking ice cream all over my seat! You are so darn clumsy! You are worse than a kid! Get out!"

"Really Perry, it is not that serious! If you get me a few wet napkins it will come right up. Your seats are leather, you know."

By now, Nancy stood, still holding the seat forward so Laura could exit the vehicle. She appeared noticeably annoyed at Perry's reaction. Finally, she casually spoke to Perry.

"Perry, I have a few cloths in the house; we can wet them, put a little detergent on them and your seats will be good as new. Let's get this ice cream in the freezer and we all can come back out and get this cleaned up. It is really not a big deal."

Perry snapped back. "To you, Mrs. Maxwell, it is not a big deal, but to me it is. I just want her clumsy behind out of my car. I will clean it up myself."

At Perry's remark, Laura angrily, and amid embarrassment exited the car. As she stooped to get out, she met her mother face to face. Nancy whispered, "You certainly got something on your hands." At her mama's remarks, Laura just gazed at her with teary eyes from the hurtful things he had said, walked past her, and went inside.

Laura continued staring at the ceiling searching the past for red flags. *Mom, doused with wisdom, and not to mention experience, tried to warn me. But we had just gotten married. I think we were married for about six months at the time. So, what was I supposed to do, run for the hills over a rebuke from spilled milk?*

Laura turned over on her side to ponder some more. The abrupt rattling of the guest bedroom doorknob startled her… she quickly jumped up at the sound.

"Laura, I'm sorry… can you please come out so we can finish talking?" Laura quickly laid back down and returned to her previous position. "Go away Perry and leave me alone… I am not coming out of this room until I have to go to work. So, you can beg until the cows come home, I am not budging!"

"Now you do know I can get in if I really want to?"

"Yeah, I know. And you do know, I still can help rid you of your dinner too, right? I mean, by now it should be waste that is ready for release. Now, we can do it the way God intended for it to come out, or I can expedite the process–the choice is yours." Laura's heart raced after her remark… she wondered if Perry had it in him to kick the door down as he had done in the past. But she was getting stronger. At least she would like to think she was. Her mother took it without one ounce of rebuttal – she just took it. *But I don't want to be like Mom. What in the world have I done to have to live like this?* Laura clutched the knife under her pillow, listened to Perry's footsteps drifting away from the door, sighed, and soon drifted off to sleep.

CHAPTER III

The next morning, Laura was awakened by Lisa and Greg's usual *'hurry up in the bathroom antics.'* She listened for Perry's movements and discovered that he had left already. She got dressed, made sure the children were off to school and drove to work. As she entered the building she caught a glimpse of Vivian strutting through the intersected corridor. Laura rolled her eyes and slowed her pace so as not to engage in communication with her. But out of Vivian's peripheral vision, she saw Laura and stopped dead in her tracks.

"Girl, did you get any sleep at all last night? You look like you sat up all night."

"What is to you if I did sit up all night."

Vivian opened her mouth to offer more smirky remarks, but Laura put her hand up and shook her head – "Nope, I'm not doing this with you today, Vivian. I am not in the mood. So, I suggest you take your tail someplace else and harass others; your odds will be better, trust me."

"Is that supposed to be a threat?"

"Call it what you want," said Laura and she walked away in the opposite direction. Down the hallway, she saw Amelia. Their eyes met and they strolled into the teachers' lounge.

"Hey Amelia, how was your evening?" Amelia answered but tried to avoid eye contact.

"It was good, what about yours?"

Laura sighed, "I've had better, let's just put it like that. Those darn kids, all they want to do is fight."

"Yeah, I hear you, mine too." Amelia continued to pretend she was doing busy work, like searching the school mail cubbies looking for mail. Laura noticed that Amelia searched the same boxes, and they were noticeably empty, but Amelia kept peeking and peering as if she believed something was inside.

Suddenly, the bell rang, alerting teachers it was time for them to report to their posts to greet arriving students. Laura could see Amelia's post from her stance. Now and then, Amelia would crack a fake smile as the children happily greeted her. *I wonder what is troubling her?* thought Laura. "Hey, Mrs. Clayton!" A student greeted–interrupting Laura's thoughts. "Oh, Good morning Thomas!" greeted Laura. She then gave Thomas a quick pat on his head and ushered him in the direction of the cafeteria. Laura continued to inconspicuously peer at Amelia, who by now appeared to wipe her eyes constantly in between student greetings. Laura thought to herself, *what could be her problem? I bet she wasn't clutching a knife all night long.*

———————

After school, and as the teachers headed outside to see the children off for home, Laura decided to speak with Amelia. As she walked toward her, she thought – *I hope she tells me what's been troubling her all day. I hope she's alright. I don't feel so bad now that I realize someone else got issues other than me – well all except that big mouth Vivian.* Amelia looked up at Laura's presence and remarked, "I meant to tell you, I like that yellow dress you have on. It's nice and airy-looking. Where did you get it?"

Laura looked down at the dress and lightly pressed it with her hands, "This old thing. I got it from Marshall's. Girl, I've had this a couple of years now, but thanks for the compliment." Amelia gave that fake smile again and waved goodbye at the children as they dashed for their parent's cars. Laura mustered up the strength to ask Amelia if she was okay.

"Hey, I've been noticing you throughout the day, Amelia, and was wondering, are you OK? Is everything alright?"

"Sure, why do you ask?"

Laura persisted, "I mean, you seemed so sad throughout the day, that's all?"

Amelia shot Laura an annoyed glance. "Um, you didn't look like you were on a cakewalk today either, so I could ask you the same question?"

Shocked at Amelia's response, Laura begin to talk, but Amelia interrupted, "Listen, I would love to carry on with this probing conversation, but Troy will be here soon to pick me up and I have to go back into the classroom to tidy up my desk before leaving." After her remark, Amelia turned on her heels and walked back into the school. Laura stood baffled. *I don't understand; on Wednesday she was comforting me, now today she's distant, moody. I don't know what to think.* Shaking her head, Laura followed Amelia but turned down a different hall to get to her classroom. She grabbed her purse, keys, and other belongings and traveled home.

In deep thought, Laura wondered what she would face when she arrived home. Would Perry be there, and if so, what kind of a mood would he be in. Laura always tried to stay one step ahead of his ghastly larks, but sometimes it seemed as if he recognized her wittiness and changed maneuvers to throw her off.

The garage door went up and there was Perry's car. *Lord, I was hoping he would not be home just yet, at least for a while anyway.* Laura reached to the back seat to retrieve her items. She then patted around under the seat to get the kitchen knife she stowed earlier that morning. She put it inside her purse and exited the car. The whiff of dinner met her nose and she immediately thought Perry was in his *'let me play nice so I can beat your behind mood.'* Lisa and Greg met her at the door hugging and yelping about how glad they were that it was finally Friday.

"Mom, Dad is cooking tacos tonight," Lisa blurted.

"She knows that, Dummy!" interjected Greg.

"Hey, hey, hey, let's stop with the name-calling, Gregory! Please learn how to treat your sister with respect. If you don't respect her, how do you think others will?" Just then, Perry appeared from the hallway of their home. Laura side glanced at him and walked briskly past, toward the guest bedroom. Perry followed while Greg and Lisa bickered about Laura's awareness of dinner.

"Laura," Perry called to her as he followed.

"All I was trying to tell you Lisa is that you think Mama is dumb – don't you know she knows what tacos smell like."

"Leave me alone Gregory; all you do is call me names; you think you are so smart!"

"I am – I'm smarter than you."

"Leave me alone!" Lisa demanded.

At the sound of Laura's name coming from Perry's peaceful sounding voice, she stopped in her tracks while switching her purse from one shoulder to the other.

"Laura, I was just hoping we could talk."

"About what this time, Perry?"

"Please," Perry interrupted, "I have something to share that is very important. Can we talk after dinner?"

Laura tilted her head slightly upward and cautiously slid her hand inside of her purse. "What is so important, Perry. Can't you tell me now?"

"Dang it, woman, I'm trying to do what's right here, can't you see that? I just want to talk. I got to make this right with you, I have to!"

Laura felt for the knife and clutched it, keeping it concealed. She then took in a deep breath and turned toward Perry.

"Okay, okay," she said while nodding her head. "We will talk after dinner, but I'm warning you, if I feel the least bit uncomfortable, the conversation ends. You got that Perry?"

Perry clapped his hands and rubbed them together. "I hear you, loud and clear. Trust me, I think you will love what I have to say." He then took a couple of steps backward before turning around to walk toward the kitchen.

Laura took in a deep breath and walked into the guest bedroom. Immediately, she closed the door and locked it. *"Lord,"* she began to pray, *"please don't let this weekend be terrible. All I want is peace, just a little peace Lord."* Laura took the knife out of her purse and placed it on the bed. She changed clothes and slipped into something comfortable. At first, she donned her favorite fuzzy socks. But she thought about what if she had to make a run for it… so she stepped quietly out of the room and walked to the master bedroom. There she went to her closet and grabbed a pair of running shoes and slipped them on. As she walked toward the kitchen, she briefly turned around and went back to the guest bedroom to get the knife. Laura wrapped the knife in a pair of socks and then slipped it behind her back wedged between her back and her sweatpants.

"Mommy!" yelled Lisa. "We are hungry, come on!"

"I'm coming, I'm coming – hold your horses as your grandmother would say" When Laura entered the kitchen; everyone was seated.

Perry gave Laura's appearance the once over and then asked. "Are you planning on going somewhere after dinner?"

"Why, Perry?"

With raised hands and shrugged shoulders Perry answers, "I'm just wondering, I see your sweatsuit and running shoes on, I just thought you might be going out after dinner, that's all."

"No," Laura responded while pulling out the chair to sit. "I'm not going anywhere." She then looked at Perry, "At least I hope not."

The Clayton family sat and enjoyed their tacos. Of course, and as usual, 12-year-old Gregory asked for seconds. During the entire time of family meal indulging, no one seemed to have any conversation to contribute. Everyone kept their heads down and consumed every bite on their plate. Even Laura seemed to enjoy her meal. Although she withstood it amid a racing heart. Now and then she would take a deep breath to allow the food to go down so that she could put another forkful into her mouth.

After the meal, Perry got up to gather the dishes and gave out orders for the children to complete their kitchen chores. Of course, bickering ensued between the two and Perry abruptly stopped it with threats of punishment. Just the sound of his voice giving commands caused alarm in Laura. She kept waiting for the punch line, a sinister remark, something that would give her enough time to make it out of the house.

"Gregory, take this trash out, while your sister puts the food away. After y'all finished, go make sure your rooms are straight. I have a surprise for the family tomorrow." Laura casually walked over to the sofa, picks up the remote, and turned to watch the news. Perry entered the family room shortly and picked up the remote to turn it off. Laura made a motion to stand, but Perry gently touched her arm. "Please, Laura, sit… I'm not telling you or demanding, I'm asking, please – sit?"

"No, thank you, I'd rather stand." Laura stood with her arms folded.

Perry nodded, "Okay, that's fine." He then looked up at his wife of 13 years. He stared for a minute. Laura unfolded her arms and placed them on her hips with her fingers facing her back. Perry began his spiel. "Remember the other night I told you that I hated how I treated you?" Laura nodded. "Well," Perry continued. "I decided to do something about it."

"Something like what, Perry."

"I'm in counseling."

"Really?" Laura inquired with raised eyebrows. "With whom?"

"Does it matter Laura?"

"You darn right it matters – what's so hard about you telling me who you are receiving counseling from?"

"Mittlings Counseling Services."

"Mittlings, who the heck are they? I've never heard of them before?"

"Yeah, yeah, I know – they are new. It was recommended to me by a co-worker of mine."

Laura became suspicious, "A co-worker? How did you manage, and that is if you did, to tell folk what you do to me, Perry? Do you expect me to believe this bull?"

Perry stood, and Laura stepped back while sliding her hands closer to her weapon.

"Relax, Sweetheart, I'm just reaching for the business card from my counselor." Perry reached for the card and passed it to Laura. She read it and the two of them sat on the sofa simultaneously. "Will I be able to sit in on some of these sessions?" asked Laura.

"Not right away. I want to be able to pour my heart out in all honesty, but the counselor did say you can join soon."

"Okay well, this sounds promising. I've been waiting for this for a long time. So, what happened today – was today the first day?" Laura asked.

"Nope, as a matter of fact, I started Wednesday. This past Wednesday. For the first 21 days – I am to report every day. That is why you have been seeing me home early. The job allows me time to go, and I don't have to report back to work afterward. So, you see, Baby, I'm trying, I really am. Will you be willing to come back to our bedroom now?"

"Perry, are you for real right now? Heck, I need some counseling too!" She sighs. "You don't realize the damage that your conduct has caused. It paralyzes me sometimes. I don't know whether I'm coming or going. Let me ask you something. Why do you treat me the way that you do? What have I done to deserve the things that you do to me? Do you realize that one day our daughter is going to get married and she is going to think that it is OK for a man to beat her, rape her and call her out of her name – she is going to think it's OK, Perry – because she has witnessed you do it over and over again. And Gregory is going to do the same thing to other women. Is that what you want?"

Perry shook his head, with tears flowing. "No, no, that is not what I want!" He then looked at Laura. "That is why I am in this counseling, I want to do better, I swear I do!"

"Well, the counseling is a start. But until I see a drastic change in you Perry, I just can't lie next to you, I just can't."

"Can we just try, Laura! I mean, I'm in counseling; can't you come back to the bedroom and try?"

Laura shook her head, 'No.' "It is too soon, Perry. You had just three days of counseling and you think everything is supposed to be hunky-dory? No, it doesn't work like that." She shook her head again, "I'm sorry, let's get through these counseling sessions first and" – she said as she pointed a finger toward her chest. "Let me see a drastic, and I mean a drastic change in your behavior, then we can discuss the bedroom." Afterward, Laura grabbed a jacket from the hall closet and walked toward the front door.

"Wait a minute, where are you going? I thought you said you weren't going out?" asked Perry.

Laura stopped at the front door, never looking back, and replied, "I'm going for a walk, Perry, is that alright with you?" Perry jumped up. "I'll join you if you don't mind."

Laura turned to face Perry, "I do mind. I want to be alone." She opened the door quickly and left the house.

———————

During her walk, Laura could not help but think of Perry's inconsistencies in turning his life around. He had attempted to change so many times before… but this time did seem different. *I can only hope he is sincere*, she thought. Laura stopped momentarily, looked around, and thought seriously about allowing Perry back into their bedroom. *'I can't, I just can't,'* she murmured, and then she continued her walk. If I bend too soon, it will interfere with any counseling he is receiving. Laura then thought about the business card Perry gave her before leaving the house. She reached into her jacket pocket, pulled out the card, and searched for a phone number. Precariously, she glanced around, then located the nearest phone booth and dialed the number.

"Mittlings Counseling Services. How may I direct your call?"

"Ma'am, my name is Laura Clayton, I'm Perry Clayton's wife. I'm wondering if you could answer a few questions for me?"

"Mrs. Clayton, it depends on the depth of your inquiry. At most, we are not allowed to share a client's information with anyone unless given permission from our clients."

"But I'm his wife," Laura explained.

"I understand, Mrs. Clayton – what exactly is your question?"

Laura took a deep breath and then asked. "Is Perry in counseling with your agency?"

"Has Mr. Clayton had any type of discussion with you in regard to our agency?"

"Yes, yes he has. In fact, we just had a discussion, and he gave me this card from your company."

"Mrs. Clayton, is Mr. Clayton with you at this moment?"

"No, he's not? Ma'am, I just want to know if he is receiving treatment from you."

"Yes, he is Mrs. Clayton and that is all I can share."

Laura nodded and thanked the representative; she then left and walked hastily back toward home.

CHAPTER IV

Laura woke early on Saturday morning. She reached into the nightstand and retrieved her journal. She began to read some entries from years past. Her journal helped her to expel her fears. Tears flowed as she read. She began to relive what she endured during her pregnancy with Lisa.

Laura remembered, vividly, running from Perry, one cool September afternoon, while four months pregnant with Lisa. Perry was on one of his rampages and had beat her the night before. After she thought he was sound asleep while taking a nap, she slipped on some clothes and quickly escaped their home and ran to a neighbor's house.

Of course, and not long after she arrived, Perry stood on the neighbor's doorstep, banging on the door, demanding that Laura come out. Carl and Sara, their friends, were close in age to Laura and Perry–would not allow Perry to come in. But Laura, who stood behind Carl, now began to pace nervously while crying and screaming, "He's not going to go away unless I come out!" But Carl, stood in front of Laura, while his wife, Sara tried to console her.

"Come on, Perry!" Carl called out to his friend. Let's not let the entire neighborhood in your business. Go on home. We will take care of Laura and bring her home once she calms down. She's pregnant man! Let her settle down."

But Perry didn't hear a word Carl said to him… He kept banging and banging until Carl finally reached for the door.

Sara shouted, "Carl, please tell me you are not about to let that fool in here!" Carl glanced back briefly and then told Sara to take Laura into another room. "I'm going to see if I can talk some sense into this man. This stuff has got to stop." Sara did as direct by Carl.

Carl opened the door. Perry stepped closer and tried to enter.

"Nope," Carl said as he put his hands up gesturing to stop Perry. "You are NOT going to bring this crap into my house. Man, what in the world is wrong with you? Your wife is pregnant! It doesn't make any sense the way that you treat her." Perry begins to pace, grabbing his head and pacing. "I just want her to come home," Perry screamed.

"For what?" Answered Carl. "So, you can beat the hell out of her again? Man, you need some serious help. You do! You have a good wife, and you want to abuse her?"

Perry stopped pacing and looked up at Carl. "Man, what is your problem?" he asked Carl. "You act as if you want her. I know what I have, I don't need you to tell me what I have! Just tell Laura to get her behind out here now so that we can go home!"

"You know what," Carl responded. "I'm about to close my door on that remark. You will not enter this house until you act like you got some sense."

Meanwhile, Sara and Laura stood in the bedroom listening to Perry's outbursts and Carl's reasoning.

"Laura, what are you going to do? You can't go on living like this? I mean, I can't tell you what to do, but something bad is bound to happen if Perry keeps acting like this." Sara then reached onto the dresser to pass Laura some tissues. She noticed the scratches and bruises on Laura's arms and neck. "What makes him so angry?" Sara asked.

"Anything, it could be anything. He doesn't like the way I make French toast, or how I made the bed, or—it doesn't have to be anything in particular at all. I don't know what I'm going to do. I'm pregnant again, maybe that's it."

Sara shook her head. "That's not it, Laura. Stop making excuses for him. I agree with Carl. Perry needs some help!"

Unexpectedly, the two women heard Perry's voice draw closer.

"I know Carl did not let that fool in here," Sara snapped. Sara got up and walked closer to the front entrance. She then stepped back and leaned against the wall to eavesdrop.

Perry was now in the living room of the Peterson's home.

"I promise," Perry reassured. "I just want to talk with her. Do you think you can get her to come out to hear what I have to say?" Perry looked at Carl with tears in his eyes as he asked.

Carl answered. "Let it be amicable… Let me see if she is willing to talk to you."

Sara quickly stepped to the bedroom where Laura sat safely. "Perry is out there, and he wants to talk to you. Are you willing to see him? You don't have to do this if you don't want to, Laura. If you ask me, I think you should leave him."

The thought of Laura's marriage dissolving was hurtful, to say the least. She looked at Sara with tear-filled eyes and whispered. "I'll see him."

Slowly, Laura walked past Sara and met Carl midway. "He's out there and wants to talk to you," Carl said to Laura. "If you want, I can be in the same room with you or… "

Laura shook her head. "No, I think I'll be fine. He's not that crazy to hit me in front of you guys, I'm sure." Laura then stepped aside and walked into the Peterson's living room. As she entered she saw Perry pacing. Once he noticed her presence he stopped and walked toward her.

"Laura, I'm sorry, so sorry. I've come to take you home." Perry then reached for Laura's arm and started toward the front door. She gently pulled away. Perry abruptly turned around.

"Come on girl, I don't have time to waste. Greg is home, and… "

"Wait a minute," Laura interrupted, "You left Greg home by himself, Perry?"

Perry snapped, "Do you think I'm a fool? No, he's not home by himself. He's only two, Laura; gosh, give me some credit."

"Well, who's watching him then?" Laura asked.

"Don't worry about that, he's being taken care of. I need you to come on home." He then leaned in and said, "You got them all up in our business." He then reached for Laura's arm, but she yanked away and turned to walk toward the room where she believed Carl and Sara were waiting.

Perry pounced. He snatched Laura by her hair and threw her to the floor. She screamed for Carl to come help but he had stepped out into the backyard. Perry began to kick Laura, he kicked her in the stomach, and she let out a scream that would seemingly wake the dead. Sara ran into the room.

"Stop it Perry, stop!" But Perry kept kicking. Laura screamed and screamed. She crumpled into the fetal position to block the blows from Perry's perilous foot.

Abruptly, Perry was propelled onto his back as Carl charged into the room and landed a blow to his head. Sara rushed to help Laura off the floor while Carl put a fierce thrashing on Perry. Carl then picked Perry up by the collar of his shirt and tossed him out of the house. He then turned to Laura and shouted, "I'm going to call the police on that idiot!"

"Noooo, please don't!" Laura screeched.

"What?" Sara yelled. "Laura that fool is going to kill you one day! Why don't you leave his good for nothing behind alone! He is not worth living with. He is going to kill you!"

Sara then looked at Carl and said, "Call the police and the ambulance too! I ain't messing with Perry. He done lost his mind!"

Laura sat, just shaking her head from left to right. "Y'all making it hard for me. You just don't know how angry he's going to get. He is going to blame this all on me. Please don't call the police, Carl, please don't!"

Carl hissed and shook his head, grabbed the phone, and called 911.

Laura continued to scan through her journal… shaking her head and dropping tears while reading line for line. *"Why, Lord, am I still here? What is keeping me here? I feel like a dog who has upset his master time and time again. Only my house is NOT my safe haven.* She then turned the journal to its cover, she scribbled on it. Tears fell from her eyes as she wrote. She gently brushed them away and kept writing. Laura then turned her attention back to perusing the contents. She came across another gory notation. Pulling the bed linens up close to her body, she nestled and began to read.

Memories soared while reading. Laura remembered her second trimester with Lisa. It was a warm Spring day and she was preparing to go to work. Perry came up with this wise idea to carpool to save money on gas. But Laura refused. And so, the trauma ensued.

"How can you say no to a simple request!" Perry barked.

"Look, I'm going on seven months pregnant, Perry. When I'm ready to leave for home, I don't want to have to wait. Now leave me alone so that I can finish getting dressed." With that remark, Laura turned around while simultaneously putting her earring in her ear.

She started toward the bathroom when Perry snatched her by the arm. He snarled. "You are going to ride with me this morning! Now get your purse and let's go!"

"Perry look… "

Before Laura could get the words out of her mouth, Perry lunged in and slapped Laura across the face. Stunned, she covered her cheek to ease the sting. She then darted toward their bedroom door, but Perry was too fast and got there before she did. His huge arm blocked the entrance.

"Perry please," Laura pleaded. "I just want to drive my car. Sometimes I don't feel good and have to leave work early." She then looked up at Perry while soothing her face. "What is so wrong with that?" she asked.

For a moment it seemed as if Perry showed a little compassion. Laura continued. "During these past few weeks, I've experienced fatigue and my feet swell from time to time. My boss has empathy and allows me to leave early. I need my own transportation, Perry, please."

Perry dropped his arm from the door's post. "So, is that why I haven't seen your car at the job on certain days?" Perry asked smugly.

"Seen my car…? Laura inquired. "What do you mean, 'Seen my car?' Have you been spying on me? Do you think… ?" Dumbfounded, Laura couldn't finish her sentences.

Perry interrupted. "… what is a man to think. I drive by your job, and you are not there. You haven't told me that you weren't feeling good or that you were tired. So, what was I to think?"

Laura dropped her hand from her stinging cheek. "You've got to be kidding me! First of all, if you paid attention to me, Perry, you would have noticed my swollen feet. And secondly, when you came home from work, where did you mostly find me – in the bed!"

Immediately after her response, Laura walked into the bedroom, got her purse, and walked out the front door. She quickened her step, climbed into her car, started the engine, and drove off. She glanced into the review mirror at her reflection. Her cheek was still red with fading fingerprints. "Darn it," she whispered. "I forgot my other earring."

CHAPTER V

Laura put the journal neatly back in its space inside of the nightstand just as Lisa loudly knocked on her door.

"Mama, whatcha doing in there? Come on out. Let's do something exciting! I want to get out of this house." Greg walked up behind Lisa and remarked,

"Daddy said he wanted to do something with us for the weekend."

Laura thought, after hearing Greg's remark.

"That's right, he did say something about that last night," Laura remarked. "Hey, listen you guys, go make sure your rooms are squared away and I will be out shortly."

"Okay!" The children shouted and then their footsteps rumbled from the door. Laura got out of bed, took a quick shower, donned a comfortable sweatsuit with her favorite Chucks, and exited the guest bedroom.

Perry sat at the kitchen table, perusing a coupon, but when he saw Laura, he directed his attention toward her. "Hey," Perry said gently. "I was thinking we could take the kids to a museum or maybe to the zoo today; what do you think?" He then glanced at the clock. "Nah," he said. It's a bit too late for the zoo, what about the museum?"

Laura joined him. "I think the kids would enjoy that. But I think I'm going to visit my mom."

Perry raised his eyebrow. "Your mom?" he replied.

"Yep," answered Laura.

"Why now," Perry asked. "I mean, don't you remember I addressed the family that I had a surprise for you guys? Laura, I wanted to do something positive for a change. Don't mess this up for me now."

"Perry, how is my visiting Mom going to mess things up? You are too anxious. Let everything work out smoothly. Time heals all wounds. You are in counseling now… so let's just see where that will lead us – okay? Besides, I think a little separation will do us both good."

"Separation?" Perry said with an amplified voice. He then stood. "You–you're not talking about staying for any length of time, are you? I mean, surely, you're not speaking of leaving me – is that where this is leading too, Laura? Because if it is, I won't… "

"…you won't what Perry?" Laura interrupted. "See, this is exactly what I'm talking about. You can't expect things to change in a blink of an eye. It won't happen that way. You have to be honest with your counselor. I need this time."

"How much time are you talking, Laura – a week, month – I mean what are we talking about here?"

"Just a few days, Perry," Laura replied.

"How many days?" Perry asked.

Laura began to get angry. "I don't know!" she shouted. "Maybe through to Tuesday. All I know is I have to get away from here for a while – just a little while, a couple of days or so."

Just then, Greg entered the kitchen and expressed that the rooms are tidy.

Perry stood. "Y'all, get your stuff together, we are going to the museum."

"Yay!" the children chimed. "Wait!" Lisa interjected. "Which one?"

"Does it matter!" Greg shot back.

Laura shot a glance at Greg, and then she looked at Perry. "While you are en route to the museum, please check your son's attitude. It is deplorable!"

Perry tapped Greg behind the head. "Let's go, knucklehead." The children gleefully followed Perry to the door.

Lisa stopped and realized that Laura was still sitting at the table. "Come on, Mom!" Laura smiled, got up, and kissed her two children. "You guys go on and have some fun. I won't be joining you." Lisa started to interrupt with her *'whys,'* but Laura gently placed her finger on Lisa's lips and finished her statement. "I'm going to visit with Grandma. I'll be back before you get out of school on Tuesday." After her statement, Laura and Perry locked eyes. He then opened the door to allow the children to leave.

Laura then visited her mother, who had also been in an abusive relationship. Her dad died a few years ago, leaving Laura's mom to struggle with paying the bills and just simple living expenses. Nancy stood about 5ft. tall. Her once youthful face had been drawn from worrying and the life she lived with her husband. Laura often helped her mother financially. She did the best that she could without making Perry privy to her monetary actions. However, Nancy was appreciative of what her daughter could do for her.

On many occasions, Laura had asked her mother to live with her, Perry, and the children. Her motive, and rightfully so, was in hopes of Perry treating her better if her mother was present in the home. But in realization, she felt deep down that Nancy's live-in arrangement would not stop a bully like Perry. Besides, Nancy had declined the offer just as many times as she was asked. For even she didn't want to look Perry in the face daily knowingly what he was doing to her daughter.

During Laura's visit, she discussed her fears with Nancy. Her mother offered suggestions. Laura had an income; she was a schoolteacher. Her mother reminded her of that. She told her that she does not have to put up with the abuse from Perry. Nancy feared that one day, Perry would strike her too hard – so much so that he would kill her.

"Mom, you keep saying that, but Perry is not that crazy. He's too proud of that job of his. He is not about to let that go."

Nancy stopped preparing dinner and turned to look at Laura. "Child, when are you going to wake up? You just sat there and told me that he struck you a few weeks ago." Nancy turned her attention back to her meal preparation, and then she said. "The next thing I know, you will be telling me that he's making you have sex when you don't feel like it."

She turned abruptly toward Laura who sat somberly with her head down. "You know men do that sort of stuff. They take it just because you are their wife – don't care how you feel or nothing – just get on top of you and do what they got to do, and we are supposed to be OK with that. And you better not say anything about it either or they…"

Before Nancy could finish her sentence, she heard sniffles coming from Laura's direction. She turned to see if Laura was crying or maybe just her nose was running.

"Are you alright over there?" Nancy asked. No answer from Laura, she just kept her head hanging low, and now and then she would wipe her eyes with the back of her hand.

Nancy stood shaking her head in dismay. She walked over to Laura and pulled out a piece of tissue from her pants pocket. "Here, take this, it's clean." She then stared at her daughter for a moment. Nancy remembered the once vibrant, jovial girl, that Laura used to be. She remembered her prom and how happy she was to go out with Perry.

Nancy saw some red flags then but stood in hopes of him changing. She felt that he was still young and had a chance to redeem himself. Nancy reminisced about Perry banging on their door in the middle of the night when he was 16 years old. His dad was raising sand with his mother; trying to pick a fight, is what Perry bellowed once we opened the door. Perry didn't like how his dad treated his mother, so why would he mistreat her daughter?

"Child, I'm going to ask you something and I want the truth, you hear me?"

"Yes Ma'am," Laura answered.

"Has he – Mph," Nancy looked away for a second to find the right words to say. She couldn't believe what she was about to ask Laura. "Has he forced you to have sex, Laura?"

Laura nodded her head up and down and continued to wipe away the evidence of sobbing.

"Mmph, mph, mph – you got to get out of there Laura. He's only going to get worse. I had to stay with your daddy. I didn't have a job, no education, and my mama, rest her soul, wasn't able to let me stay at her house, not with children. What are you going to do?"

"Mama, I don't know what I'm going to do. That's why I came here, I guess, to get some understanding. I know you went through it with daddy, but I didn't know how bad it was for you."

Nancy responded with teary eyes. "Girl, it was rough. There were times, he would run me out of the house in my slip at night. I mean it was cold out those doors. But at the time, I didn't care. I'd rather stand out on that porch and shiver than take another one of those blows that night."

"I remember one night; I ran outside to get away from his hatefulness. I was sitting on the front porch just crying my eyes out – didn't have no place to go. I looked over at the dog we had, old Shaggy – do you remember, Shaggy?"

Laura nods, "Yes."

Nancy continues, "Well I looked at Shaggy and he peeped at me with those glowing eyes from his little old doghouse. That dog looked at me as if to say, 'He got you too?' I was looking pitiful, and the dog was looking sad too." Nancy then paused, and then she said, "Laura, you don't have to take Perry's mess. I'm begging you to find some help – please get out of there."

"And go where Mama?"

"You can stay here! I ain't got much, but at least it's peaceful – ain't nobody knocking me upside my head no more."

Laura lifted her head and responded. "I would love to come here and stay. But I don't want to pull Lisa and Greg out of school. And besides, Perry would be here every day or calling me every day begging us to come back home."

Laura then shook her head from left to right indicating 'No' to her mother's request. She got up from sitting, to get a glass of water. She gulped it down and turned to face her mom. "I just need this break. If you don't mind, I would like to stay for a few days."

Nancy nodded and then replied, "You can stay for as long as you like. Don't worry about Perry coming here or calling. The policeman can handle unwanted visitors and I surely don't have to answer my phone."

Nancy went back to preparing dinner. She peeped at Laura, "You hungry?"

Laura answers, "Famished."

Nancy smiled in response, "Well, dinner will be up shortly. We will get our bellies full, and discuss your situation further, cause I'm telling you, Perry Clayton is NOT going to let up. It will take an act of God before he changes, and that's the truth!"

CHAPTER VI

Laura stayed an extra day with her mother then she headed home. She felt empowered and pondered on some of the suggestions her mother rendered. Laura thought deeply about living life without Perry. There would be peace like none she has experienced in a long time. As she drew close to her neighborhood, she saw a for sale sign in the yards of some pretty nice homes. *"I could certainly afford that,"* she thought while slowly driving passed the houses. *"Mmm, I don't know. Maybe I'll give him some time. After all, he is in counseling. And surprisingly, he didn't try to bother me while I visited Mom."* Laura soon arrived home. Greg and Lisa scurried to the car to greet her.

"Mama! You're home!"

"Wow, it's nice to be missed," Laura said as she looked down at Lisa and Greg while receiving their hugs. She then caught a glance toward the garage door to see if Perry's car was in sight. She realized that her gaze stood awkward because there is no way, Perry would leave the children alone.

"Daddy didn't cook tonight Mama," Greg blurted, "We had pizza, but it was good though." Greg smiled after his remark and let go of his mother's hand. Then he walked toward the garage and entered the kitchen.

Laura and Lisa soon followed. The house was quiet except for small chatter from a TV commercial. Laura placed her keys on the key rack and noticed from the kitchen that Perry sat slouched on the sofa in the family room. She felt in her spirit that he was aware of her presence but dared not interrupt whatever was keeping him occupied.

"Daddy, Mama's home," Greg screeched. Perry never acknowledged his wife's presence. Laura knew she might stand to be in a little trouble, so she scurried for the back door, but Perry pounced before she could lift her hand to open the door. He grabbed her by the hair and dragged her to the family room where he had sat, pretending to be engaged in the TV commercials. Grunting and squirming, Laura managed to stay on her feet, while holding her hair by the roots to lessen the pain. Greg and Lisa rushed to their mother's rescue. But they were no match for Perry's tough grip. He swiped at the children and demanded they go to their rooms.

"No!" Greg shouted. "Let Mama, go, Daddy; she ain't done nothing to you! She just got back home!"

"Stop it, Daddy!" Lisa screamed. "You're hurting her!"

The children's cries fell on deaf ears. Perry was destined to harm Laura. But why? The children continued to cry and scream for their daddy to stop but to no avail. He wouldn't listen. He had just completely lost his mind! Lisa paced the floor and continued to beg for her daddy to let her mother go. She couldn't bear to watch him mistreat her mom. She paced in a hurried, nervous fashion, peeking now and then to witness her daddy's intentions.

Suddenly, a loud thud sounded from the living room amid the TV chatter. Greg skipped over the sofa, while Lisa ran toward the noise. There lay Laura, face down on the floor. The children ran to her aid.

"What did you do to her!" Lisa screamed. She then screamed at Greg to call 911. "Mama," Lisa called out to her, but Laura did not move. Lisa tried to turn her mother over to get a look at her face, but her 10-year-old small frame could barely budge her mother's 210 lb. body. Greg rushed back into the room.

"The ambulance is on the way!" He then turned around in bewilderment.

"Where is Daddy?" He ran to the garage and shouted.

"He's gone! I can't believe he is going to just leave like that!"

Lisa got up to get a wet cloth for Laura's head.

"What the heck did he do to her?" asked Lisa. "Did you see what happened?"

She got the cloth and rushed back toward her mother while waiting on Greg's response.

Greg began to sob. Lisa looked up in between dabbing the side of her mom's head. "Greg, what happened? We have to be able to tell the ambulance people when they get here."

Between sniffles, Greg spoke. "He just dragged her over here, and… " He began to cry again.

"And what Greg, what did he do to her? I can't get her to wake up! What did Daddy do?"

Greg calmed himself for a moment, and said, "He just scooped her up like she was nothing… I thought he was going to throw her on the couch or something."

Lisa covered her open mouth with her hand, and the tears began to stream from her eyes.

Greg continued. "He just slammed her to the floor!" Greg shook his head in disbelief as he relived Perry's atrocity. "He just threw her to the floor."

Lisa finally spoke. "Call Grandma. I don't want to stay here with Daddy another night." Greg stood still babbling.

"Call Grandma, Greg!" Lisa shouted.

———————

Laura's injuries landed her in the hospital because of Perry's outrage. She suffered a broken arm and a concussion. Her mother decided to visit her but didn't realize the extent of Laura's condition. She wanted to check on her after Laura's visit but thought she'd wait until invited.

Nancy never thought she would answer the phone and hear the anguish in her grandson's voice – especially so soon. She wanted to believe that the short stay would provide some peace between Perry and Laura, but somehow, things turned out for the worst. Per Laura's conversations and her demeanor during the visit, Nancy stood certain that her baby girl was in serious trouble, but not to this extent. She could only hope and pray that Laura would come to her senses and realize that a life full of strife and abuse is not worth living.

"Ok, Greg, I need you to – Greg, baby, calm down and tell me if Laura is okay."

"No, Grandma, that's what I've been trying to tell you, she's not OK! Daddy,–Da -addy…" Greg continued to cry and had a hard time getting his words out. Lisa jumped up from tending to Laura and snatched the phone from an emotional Greg.

"Grandma," a somber Lisa calls out. "Daddy slammed Mama to the floor for no reason."

Nancy gasped, "Oh my Goodness – is she ok? Can she talk?"

"No, Grandma, I can't get her to wake up. The ambulance is on its way," Lisa mumbled amid sniffles. As soon as Lisa got those words out of her mouth, the ambulance's sirens purred in the distance.

"They're coming – they're coming," Greg screeched.

"Grandma, I gotta go – the ambulance is getting closer, and I want to be able to tell them what happened," Lisa stated briefly.

"Lisa, wait!" Nancy shouted, "Where is Perry?"

By now Lisa had walked to the window peering for the para-medics. "I don't know Grandma – I don't know where he is." She sees the flashing lights. The paramedics pull into the driveway and park. A man and a woman jump out and run toward the front door of the home. "Grandma they are here – I'll call you back," Lisa said quickly and clicked the receiver off, and opened the door for the medical personnel. "She's over here," Lisa pointed and simultane-ously led them to her mother who lay unconscious on the floor.

"How long has she been out?" the paramedic asked.

Greg shouted before Lisa could answer, "Ever since I called 911!"

The medical assistant lifted Laura's eyelids and shined his flashlight into her eyes. The other paramedic checked her pulse and vitals. The female assistant looked at the children and said, "We need to take her in." She then glances around while her partner calls in Laura's diagnosis to the hospital. "Is there anyone here with you guys?"

"No, Lisa answered. "My daddy is gone. He did this to her – and he just left." After Lisa made her statement, she walked to the kitchen table and slumped into a chair. The female paramedic followed Lisa.

She sighed and responded, "Sweetheart, we don't want to leave you guys here alone and we have to get your mother out of here as quickly as we can. Do you have a trusting neighbor that you could stay with or any relative that is close by?"

Lisa sat with tears streaming, and then she said, "I'm sure Grandma is on her way, we called her, and she said she would come." By then the other paramedic came back inside with the gurney in tow.

"Right now, sweetie, we need to get your mom some help – and now. But at the same time, we have to make sure you are safe as well."

Neither Greg nor Lisa offered any solution. The female assistant called the police and explained the situation. Meanwhile, they loaded

Laura's lifeless body onto the gurney and started out the door. As they placed her into the ambulance, a police car pulled up. Lisa still sat dazed; Greg paced and cried. Just as the ambulance's loud arrival purred, it sped away with the same. Two officers tapped lightly on the front door.

Greg ran to the door and opened it. "Are you going to put my daddy in jail?" Greg shouted.

The policeman entered the home and glanced cautiously around, and then one of them answered Greg. "No, little fellow, not right now. We are just here until your grandmother arrives. She is coming right?"

The children nodded. Greg decided to call his grandmother again to get a precise time of her arrival. But there was no answer.

"She must be on her way because she did not pick up," Greg responded. The policemen nodded.

Shortly after, Nancy arrived. She thanked the officers for staying, briefly answered a few questions regarding Perry, and then gathered the children so they could go to the hospital and check on Laura. As she drove she peered in the back seat at the children. Lisa sat quietly while wiping tears from her eyes. Greg possessed an angry expression. Every now and then he would catch a glimpse of his grandmother's stolen glances and he'd look away. Finally, they pulled into the emergency room's parking lot, parked, and bolted for the sliding doors. Lisa and Greg stood aloof as Nancy queried Laura's whereabouts.

Laura can do better; she must do better. Those words slipped from Nancy's lips as she and the kids walked toward Laura's hospital room.

"My baby, oh my goodness, what on earth did he do to you?" Nancy gently caressed Laura's hand. She then propped and fluffed the pillows to assure Laura's comfort. Laura squirmed uneasily and slowly opened her eyes. She witnessed Nancy's presence and turned away from her mother allowing the tears to escape unseen. Nancy patted her daughter's hand. "It's OK, baby – let it out. Don't hold that pain in, let it out."

"Mama," Laura whispered with her head still turned away from her mother.

"It's OK, Laura, honey, I'm here, and I am not leaving your side. Take it easy."

Laura managed to whisper again. "The kids… "

"Shhhh, don't go fretting about them. They are doing just fine. I brought them with me for a brief period, do you want to see them… they are sitting quietly in the hall."

"No – mph – mph, I don't want them to see me like this."

"I think that is a good idea. This has been a horrible ordeal for them to witness."

Laura began to turn her head from side to side, crying and wincing from the pain.

She mouthed, "Perry." Anger arose inside of Nancy, and she tried very hard not to let it surface to the human eye. She spoke as softly and as gently as she knew how as she kissed Laura's forehead.

"Honey, Perry is in jail." Laura frowned and immediately she exposed a frightful disposition. "Laura, I know you don't like it and I realize that you are afraid. But once that baby called 911, it was all over. The police caught up with him off highway 13. He's in custody now."

As soon as those words left Nancy's mouth, a social worker, flanked by Laura's doctor and police officer walked into the room.

The officer tipped his hat toward Nancy and walked toward Laura's bedside. The doctor and social worker followed. "Mrs. Clayton, I would like to ask you a few questions if you are up to talking with me." Laura's eyes darted from the social worker to the doctor and then to Nancy. Laura extended her hand toward her mother and Nancy took her position back at Laura's bedside.

The policeman nodded in agreement and proceeded with the questionnaire. "What can you tell me about this evening if anything?"

Laura tried to sit up, but the doctor gestured for her to lie back down. "All I remembered is–I came home, the kids greeted me outside and… " She began to massage her forehead as if to prompt her thoughts. "I remember hanging my keys on the key rack and then running for the door."

"Mrs. Clayton, why did you run for the door. Was Mr. Clayton chasing you?"

Laura looked up at the officer and answered, "I don't know why I ran. Something just didn't feel right. He was sitting on the couch and then the next thing I know–he's grabbing my hair."

"When you say, 'grabbing your hair,' was it in a playful manner or… " Laura looked at the policeman then rolled her eyes away from him. She thought to herself, *does it look like he playfully grabbed my hair?*

The policeman shifted his weight from one side to the other. "Mrs. Clayton, I understand how you may feel about these questions, but I have to get pertinent details to properly charge Mr. Clayton. So, to the best of your ability, please answer my previous question. Laura then used her fingers to beckon the police officer to come closer to her. He did. She tilted her head downward, and slowly lifted her hand to point to an obvious injury allegedly done by Perry.

The police officer responded, "I see." Laura then looked at the police officer with tear-filled eyes and said, "I don't remember anything else. I'm sorry."

"That's quite all right, you've done a great job so far; however, I have one more question for you. Would you be willing to press charges against Mr. Clayton?"

Laura's lower lip trembled. Her eyes were full of dripping teardrops. She then looked toward Nancy who stood holding her hand. Nancy gave a look of sheer confidence accompanied by a slight nod. Laura then turned to look at the officer. "Yes sir," she said. "But I am afraid, of what he may do next." She reached for some tissues. "All I want right now is peace – peace for me and my children. That's all I want, and if pressing charges will give us that – then so be it."

The officer closed his notepad and explained to Laura the procedures that would soon follow. Soon afterward, he left the room. The social worker walked toward Laura's bed.

"Mrs. Clayton, I realize that answering those questions was a lot to endure, but you will soon be leaving the hospital and I want to share some safety guidelines with you if that is alright?" Laura nodded, indicating 'Yes.'

The social worker began her spiel on domestic violence and all it entails. "Laura," she began, "how long have you and your husband been married?"

"Um, pretty close to 13 years. We got married shortly after we discovered that I got pregnant."

"Mmm, okay, I just understood you to say, 'You got pregnant.' I hope you are not blaming yourself for any of this madness. You didn't get pregnant by yourself. And I'm assuming it was consensual?"

"Oh, yes, then it was… "

"The social worker interrupted, "Then it was? Is your sexual relationship with your husband not consensual at the present?"

Laura shifted her body to make herself more comfortable and then responded. "Lately, it has been a nightmare. Most times I went along with what he wanted to avoid trouble."

After jotting down notes of Laura's conversations, the social worker then asked. "Do you plan to continue to live with your husband, Mrs. Clayton?"

"I mean after this fiasco; I might as well leave. I don't know what he will do next. I mean, he often apologizes but turns right back around, weeks – months later, and does it again. It's getting worse." She sighed and turned to wipe away tears. "I don't want the children to grow up without a dad." Laura bit her bottom lip. "I just want it to stop. I want peace, that's all I want."

The social worker notated again and then remarked. "Mrs. Clayton, I must warn you that leaving an Intimate Partner Violence Relationship is… "

Laura interrupted, "… I'm sorry, leaving a what?"

"An Intimate Partner Violence Relationship is what domestic violence is referred to today. What I was about to say is, that it can be very risky and even dangerous if you don't have a plan in place. You also must recognize the signs – red flags so to speak."

"Ma'am, we are so past the red flags. I saw them. I just ignored them." Laura then looked at Nancy. "My mother went through the same thing," Laura said and continued. "She had to stay, but I don't. I just don't want my children to grow up without a dad."

"Mrs. Clayton, you keep repeating yourself. Something has to be done. You will have to have a plan in place before the next attack. And trust me it is on the horizon." The social worker took in a deep breath. "I'm going to be really frank with you – if you don't get some sort of safety strategies in place soon – your babies may grow up without a mom. You don't deserve this type of behavior."

Nancy interrupted, "That's what I've been trying to tell her." The social worker acknowledged Nancy's comment and then directed her attention back to Laura.

"Do you guys share a bank account?" The social worker asked but decided to take another approach. "Let me ask you this first; do you know in your hearts of hearts if you are going to stay. Because that answer alone will determine your future steps for safety."

"I can honestly tell you this," Laura replied. "Right now, at this moment, and once I'm released, I'm going home with my mother. Does that answer your question?"

"Yes, it does. Now we can put some strategic safety plans into place to protect you once Mr. Clayton is released. I really wish you and women in your situation would pay attention to those red flags. I know that domestic violence can be subtle at times, but there are signs. Sometimes, and in many cases, we have invested so much of our time into a relationship that signs and or red flags are easily overlooked.

"Nonetheless, and looking at the situation you are currently facing, we are far beyond red flags, we are in survival mode." The social worker reached into her briefcase and pulled out a list of safety strategies for Laura. "Here, please read over this document very carefully. Once you are released, please put these strategies into action." Afterward, the social worker picked up her belongings and started for the door. Nancy followed.

"Thank you so much for your words of wisdom. I can only pray she pays attention to what you were saying. This has been going on for years, and Lord knows, I don't want to lose my daughter."

"Unfortunately, Ma'am, this kind of behavior only escalates if not stopped. But there are survival stories, and Laura can have one too." The social worker then looked at her watch. "I must go now; I have another client across town. Stay safe, and I will keep in touch to see what Laura's plans are for safety." With that, the social worker left.

Nancy turned around to face Laura who lay browsing through the documents. *That's a good sign.* Nancy thought to herself. "Laura, honey, I'm going to get ready to go. I'll be back tomorrow, Lord willing." Laura looked up rendering a faint smile. Nancy grabbed her stuff, kissed Laura on her forehead, and started for the door.

"Mom!" Laura blurted. "I love you!"

"Oh, Laura, I love you too!"

"If it is not too much trouble would you please bring my journal when you come tomorrow – it is on my nightstand in the guest bedroom."

"Sure thing Laura, you get some rest now." Nancy lightly tapped the door as she left. Tears filled her eyes as she made her way down the corridor toward the elevators. She tried desperately to disguise her tears; pretending that her allergies were acting up.

"Is Mama going to be OK?" Lisa asked.

"Yeah, did she ever wake up?" asked Greg. Swiping at his nose and wiping tears away, Nancy quickly answered the children as she rushed down the corridor toward the elevator.

This mess is just a vicious circle – a vicious circle is what it is. Lord, I pray that Greg and Lisa never have to go through such violence. Nancy pressed the elevator button. The doors opened with a slight chime. They entered and disappeared behind the gentle shutting of steel.

CHAPTER VII

THE EARLY EIGHTIES

Many years had passed now since the terrible beating of Laura Clayton. Perry remained in and out of the prison system. He also did not want to give up on his marriage, despite his horrible demeanor. His children no longer wanted to have anything to do with him. Nancy was older now, but Laura and the children are indebted to taking care of her. Why not? She had been there for them through thick and thin. Laura's indebtedness to her mother led her to make some enormous changes.

Nancy moved in with Laura. It proved to be another safe haven for Laura and the children. Perry wouldn't dare cause any more trouble that would land him in jail. He's gotten older too and has had his fair share of a one-room condo. Besides, whenever he did visit and signaled an inkling of trouble, Nancy was sure to dial 911.

Lisa finally made up her mind about what she wanted to do in life. With her mother's guidance, she decided to join the military. Greg, on the other hand, had taken job after job. Nothing seemed to suit his taste. He was argumentative, unpunctual, and thought he knew it all. He had even been back and forth living with Laura or Nancy, it didn't matter, whoever could tolerate his toxic persona, that's where he tarried. Finally, his luck ran out with his mom and grandmother, and he was left to manage life on his own.

Lisa stood determined to make something of herself. She imagined Laura's words ringing in her ears when she started basic training. "You go out there and do the very best that you can do, Lisa. You can do it; I know that you can." Lisa stood in deep thought, as she lay in the prone position waiting on the tower to give instructions on when to fire her weapon. She was now in basic training and took to heart everything Laura had taught her.

"Ooooh, if Mama could see me now!" she thought as she lifted her weapon to fire. Each time a target popped in Lisa's visual, it flopped from the lead of her weapon. Lisa couldn't wait until evening when all the activities of the day were completed so she could write to Laura and tell her about her accomplishments.

Lisa was so proud of herself… and rightfully so, because no one in that small town in North Carolina thought she would make it through Basic Training. Lisa thought back on how Laura would push her to make up her mind to find out what she wanted to be in life. She would say, "Girl, you better get it together, because I am not going to take care of any grown adults." And then she would say as she walked off, "And you better make your own money! Don't depend on no man." Sometimes Laura's voice faded as she walked into another room still talking, "And if a man raises his hand to hit you, get out of there and don't look back." Lisa smiled, and said out loud, "That ole Mama knows she is something else."

––––––––

The first eight weeks of basic training were soon over and afterward, Lisa had to prove her skills in logistics, which would be her primary Military Occupation Specialist (MOS). Lisa enjoyed the Advancement Individual Training (AIT), mainly, because the restrictions were loosened, and she got a chance to venture throughout the military base and explore. Secondly, she learned about her new job and could not wait until she reached the finish line and traveled to her permanent party. There she could let her hair down and have fun, amid being a great soldier, which was her sole desire.

Lisa studied hard at AIT. She made good grades and passed all required tests. In doing so, she was promoted from Private to Private First Class (PFC). She was able to skip a grade passed her peers because of a few college courses she took before enlisting in the Army.

Time crept on and soon it was time for Lisa to get a break. She was going home! She could not wait to sport her new body, her rewards obtained throughout training, and to shut the mouths of the nay-sayers. *Yeah*, she thought, *I can't wait for y'all to see me now, and to hear my success stories. Shoot, some of you are still in that small town doing nothing. I'm glad Mama, clamped down on me. She made me do something – make something out of myself.*

Fall stood right around the corner and Lisa realized it to be bittersweet to go home. The Army gave all the soldiers who completed Basic Training and AIT, leave time before reporting to their permanent duty station. As she packed, she thought about Greg. At first thought – it would be nice to see her brother. But she had hoped that he had changed and not make her visit one she or her mom and grandmother would regret. She wanted this trip home to be special. It had been a long rough two and a half months and Lisa felt she deserved some R & R (Rest and Recreation).

Chatter from other soldiers packing and discussing their R & R plans soared throughout the bay area where Lisa spent two and a half months with other trainees. She abruptly wiped at her face and searched her locker for small miscellaneous items. She tossed them in her luggage. Her uniform hung on the locker's door. She swiped at it to knock off any unwanted lint. Suddenly, someone yelled in the hallway. "Did someone call for a taxi?" The voice drew closer, "Yo, Clayton, did you call for a taxi?"

Lisa scrambled to retrieve her luggage and uniform while answering the soldier, "Yeah, yeah, I did call for one."

The female soldier added, "Well it's here, I suggest you hurry up before someone snags it. Here, let me help you." The soldier began helping Lisa gather her things and they both raced to the barrack's exit.

Lisa realized that she was missing something – something extremely important and she shouted, "Wait!" She patted herself and said, "Oh no!"

"What is it," the other soldier asked.

Frantically, Lisa answered, "Did you see a notebook, on the bunk?"

"Yeah, I grabbed it for you," the soldier remarked. "Here." She gives Lisa the booklet and they race toward the taxi. Out of breath, Lisa tosses her luggage in the trunk of the taxi and takes her seat in the back. She adjusts her clothing, takes a deep breath, and clutches the notebook.

The ride to the airport seemed extremely long. She could not wait to get home and see everyone. She thought about Greg, Grandma, and Laura. Some thoughts of Perry existed but she quickly shut them out. She hated her dad, for how he treated her mother. Lisa thought, *Greg and I shouldn't have ever witnessed the things we've seen done to our mom and by the hands of Daddy."*

Once Lisa arrived at the airport, she found the area where she was to board. She waited and soon she boarded the plane. Once seated, Lisa prepared herself for takeoff. As the plane's engine roared she felt the sensation of pressure pressing her body against the seat.

Once in flight, the plane jolted a little and then settled into a smooth nonturbulent flight. Lisa reached into her carry-on bag and retrieved the booklet. She flipped through the pages and began journaling. She wrote about the fun she had in basic training. She wrote about the guys she met and how they treated her. She didn't want to miss any details about her newfound journey. When questions were asked – and there will be numerous ones, she wanted to be ready.

———————

Lisa soon landed in Raleigh, North Carolina. The anticipation of her excitement was unimaginable. She could not wait to deplane and greet her mom, grandmother, and maybe Greg – she wasn't too sure if he would show. Nonetheless, his absence or presence could not extinguish the feelings she felt inside. Lisa finally made it to the carousel, retrieved her luggage, and rushed past other travelers to greet her folk.

As she turned the bend, she began weaving and waving her head from side to side searching heartily for her family. Finally, a familiar smile and an energetic wave pierced the air and Lisa almost stumbled when she ran to meet them. She dropped her bags and ran into Laura's arms. Nancy stood just a few feet away with her hands folded lowly in front of her body. Her eyes watered and when it was her turn, she grabbed Lisa and smile so broadly. Nancy gently pushed Lisa away from her to gaze at her body.

"Girl, you look some kind of good," Nancy beamed. "Turn around and let me look at you," Nancy demanded as she assisted Lisa in her roundabout spin. "Mmph. Mmph, Mmph," Nancy grunted, "The Army certainly agrees with you, Lisa! I'm so proud of ya, baby – you look good!" Laura agreed with delight, and they helped Lisa with her luggage and started for the car.

The hour and a half ride home seemed like forever. Lisa was hoping that some of the neighbors would be out and about once she arrived. She wasn't expecting anybody to give her a welcome home hoopla – she just wanted them to see that she has made something out of her life. As the car rolled up on the lumpy driveway, sure enough, there were some of her neighbors outside, some piddling around in their yards and some standing as if waiting for someone.

"Wow," Lisa spoke, "Mama, did you tell anyone about me coming home?"

Laura, smiled, "I certainly did! I told anyone who would listen." She then added, "Even the naysayers!"

Nancy chuckled amid grunts as she exited the car, and then she responded once she caught her breath, "I know that's right! Folk is something else. They love to see you doing bad, so they can have something to talk about. Truth be told, they need to sweep around their own front door before they try to sweep around mine, or anybody else's."

Lisa and Laura laughed at Nancy's remarks while taking Lisa's bags out of the car. A male neighbor who Lisa went to school with, saw Lisa and yelled out to her. "Lisa, girl is that you?" He covered his mouth with one hand while attempting to pull up his pants by the crotch with the other. He began to sidewalk his way toward the women's direction.

Nancy put her hand up. "Nope, we don't need any company DeShawn. You can just turn around and finish doing what you were doing."

DeShawn stopped walking and then responded, with both hands in the air, "Mrs. Nancy, I was just going to help y'all carry those bags inside. They look mighty heavy!"

Laura interjected, speaking over her shoulder, never acknowledging him visually. "We got it – don't need any help." And then she picked up her pace and said, "Y'all come on! He sees how pretty Lisa is looking and he's about to break his neck to get over here."

Nancy chimed in, "I know – with his 'I don't want to work,' mooching off of his mama, lazy, sorry behind self."

Lisa laughed so loud that she had to stop and bend over to get her composure. She lifted her head and looked in Nancy's direction, "Whatcha say, Grandma?" Lisa said, while still laughing.

Nancy responded, "You heard what I said, and I meant every word." She then stopped walking, glanced in DeShawn's direction, and whispered to Lisa, "Girl, he put the *S* in sorry, that's how lazy he is." Lisa burst out laughing again, and they all staggered on into the house with gleeful hearts.

Once Lisa entered the home she dropped her baggage and stared around. "It looks really nice in here Mama." She then trotted to her old bedroom.

Laura yelled out, "I didn't do anything to your room – Mom and I just cleaned it a little. It could use a paint job, but I'll get around to it."

Lisa stood gazing around, and responded to Laura, "It looks good, Mama! I'm just glad to be home – so glad." Lisa retrieved her bags and began putting some of her stuff away. Laura entered the bedroom as Lisa unpacked.

"Wow," Laura said in amazement. "Your Army uniform is a sight to behold. I bet you look so good in it." Laura then turned toward Lisa, "Will you wear it to church this Sunday, I mean, are you allowed to?"

Lisa answered, "Sure, in fact, it is encouraged to wear our uniform on special occasions." She then turned and greeted her mother with a smile and said, "And what better place, to wear it than at church!"

They hugged and walked back into the family room to catch up on lost time.

Nancy peeped around to acknowledge their entrance and said, "It's about time you two come to join me." She then tapped the space beside her. "Come, my beautiful granddaughter, tell me all about your adventure, and don't leave out the men!"

"Grandma!" Lisa shouted.

"What? How do you think you got here!" They chuckled and Lisa began her spiel. Now and then, Nancy or Laura would interject with, 'Girl weren't you scared?' And 'Better you than me, I don't think I could have handled that.'

After Lisa's repertoire of military events, the family's focus changed and shifted toward Perry and Greg.

Lisa put her journal down which she referred to from time to time when discussing her Army adventures and asked about her dad.

"So Mom, how is Dad? I can't believe I'm asking about him as I truly hate his guts. But I guess the excitement of being home sort of made things a little easier to at least find out how he's doing. I don't really care but…"

Nancy gave Lisa a stern look, then looked at Laura. Laura glanced back at Nancy, swallowed hard, and interrupted Lisa's remark.

"Sweetheart, first of all, I don't want you to hate Perry, his guts, or anything about him. He's a sick man. He comes around from time to time."

"Are you still seeing him, Mom?"

Laura interrupted, "Hold on, now I said he comes around from time to time but I'm not sleeping with him."

Lisa responded, "But Mom, that could be so dangerous!" Lisa then pointed to the floor in front of her. She spoke with watered eyes. "It seems like it was yesterday when I saw you laying there, motionless. Mom, that was a scary time for me and Greg. Who knows, that's probably why he's half-cocked now." Lisa then repositioned herself on the sofa. She placed a knee on the chair and left her other foot to dangle relaxingly on the floor. "Where is Greg? No one has spoken about him yet?"

Nancy cleared her throat, "He's in jail."

Laura added to Nancy's comment, "Yep, that boy, I don't know what to think of him. He just wants to do what he wants to do and disregard any law or obligation. He's just like his daddy. I can't deal with him anymore."

"That explains his absence when you guys picked me up. I mean – I didn't care one way or the other. I just wanted to come home and see you guys." Lisa then got up and walked into the kitchen. She got a banana. She peeled it and began to take a bite when the doorbell rang. "I'll get it. I'm up anyway," Lisa expressed between bites. "It's probably DeShawn," Lisa added and then opened the door. To her surprise, Perry greeted her with a bouquet of flowers. Speechless, Lisa turns abruptly to look at Laura and Nancy.

"Mom, really?"

Laura motioned to get up out of her seat. "Really what?" She said as she made her way toward the front door. She then pulled at her blouse to make a neat impression and said, "Perry, what are you doing here?" Perry walked passed her, looked at Lisa, and greeted Nancy. She responded with a slight nod, and then he turned his attention back to Laura.

"What do you mean – what am I doing here. Didn't you say Lisa was coming home today?"

"Ah, yeah, I did," Laura responded and then stepped closer to him and whispered, "You were supposed to call first!"

By now Lisa strolled back to the family room and seated herself beside Nancy.

Perry whispered back, "Oh! My bad." Laura reached for the flowers, but Perry snatched them away from her. "These ain't for you, they're for Lisa."

Laura snatched them back, "You better let me put them in some water or they will certainly have a very short lifespan."

Perry grimaced sheepishly and walked into the family room. He looked at Lisa and said, "Boy, you are all grown up now. How did they treat you out there at Fort Dix?"

Lisa looked up at her daddy. Finishing up the last bite of her banana, she got up, walked past Perry, and spoke softly, "It was okay."

Perry turned to follow Lisa, "Is that all? It was ok?"

After dropping the peel in the garbage. Lisa turned toward Perry, "Yep Dad, it was okay."

She then stepped to one side of him and headed toward her bedroom. She heard Perry's footsteps approaching, and she quickly closed her bedroom door. Perry put his hands in the air as if he'd been told to do so. He stepped backward, and then turned and walked toward the family room. He took a seat across from Nancy and Laura.

"Man, talking about disrespect! I thought the Army was supposed to instill some discipline into these children. She came back worse than I could imagine."

Nancy responded, "That girl is just fine. She is focused and is making something of herself. Something you ought to be proud of."

"I am proud of her Mrs. Nancy. All I wanted to do is come and see her."

Laura interrupted, "You should have called like I told you to. But no, Perry, you still want to do things your way. That girl has not forgiven you yet."

Perry clapped his hands together and said, "I guess not. You are probably feeding her full of bull each time you get a chance."

Laura extended one hand in the air and got up from the sofa. "That's it, get out!"

Perry jumped to his feet, "Get out? I just got here!"

"I don't care!" Laura screeched through gritted teeth, "Get out, and I mean now!"

Perry looked over at Nancy, who by now had the phone in her hand, and fingers positioned to dial 911. He rolled his eyes and walked out, slamming the door.

Angrily, Laura grabbed the flowers from the vase, opened the front door, and was about to toss them toward Perry, but Nancy rose to her feet in a flash, grabbed the flowers, and quickly closed the front door.

"Mm, Mm, Girl, don't do that. Don't throw the flowers out the front door."

Angrily, Laura turned toward Nancy and shouted, "What do you expect for me to do with them, Mama!"

Nancy strolled toward the back of the kitchen, looked at Laura, and said, "Throw these suckers out the back door!"

CHAPTER VIII

Lisa's leave time from the Army seemed to be more fleeting than she had anticipated. She visited with a few high school classmates, attended a nightclub or two, and planned to use the rest of the time to spend with Nancy and Laura. As she sat in the bedroom folding laundry to pack away, Lisa couldn't help but notice her military uniform, all pressed and decorated with awards she achieved from basic training and AIT. *Wow,* she thought, *I promised Mom, I would wear my uniform with her to church.* Lisa sighed and folded another piece of laundry. *'Oh well, there will be more Sundays to come. I'm sure I can wear it then.'* She chuckled to herself and said, *"I sure had a good time at that new club on Broad St. That's why I couldn't get up in time to make it to church."* Shaking her head, she put the last piece of clothing into her suitcase and zipped it shut. She reached inside the closet to retrieve her garment bag. She secured her uniform and then glanced around the room to ensure nothing was missing.

Suddenly the phone startled her, and she quickly searched the room to find the receiver. Oh wow, it's SFC FISHER! "Hello," Lisa answered happily.

"Hey there, soldier. I saw your note where you stopped by – I hate that I missed you. So how was your tour with Uncle Sam? Did you enjoy yourself – meet anybody important, other than the drill sergeants breathing down your neck?"

Lisa laughed and responded, "Sergeant Fisher it was amazing! Thank you so much for telling me to practice running, push-ups, and sit-ups too. I did really well with all of the physical stuff!"

"Great! I'm glad to hear that! Listen, do you think you will have time to come back through to see me. I have a proposition for you."

With a frown, Lisa inquired, " Proposition? What's up?"

Fisher switched the receiver from one ear to the other... He gently bit his bottom lip and answered Lisa while he softly tapped a pencil on the desk. "I have someone I want you to meet – and that is if you are not spoken for already."

Lisa moved items on her bed aside and sat down, "Who?" She asked.

Still tapping his pencil, Fisher responded, "My brother will be in town tomorrow. He's going through a rough time – you know, with his wife..."

Abruptly, Lisa interrupted, "His wife! Sergeant Fisher, I'm not interested in talking to no married man! Who do you think I am?" Lisa then got up and started pacing.

Fisher stopped tapping and switched the receiver again, "No – No – No," he sighed loudly and continued, "That did not come out right! Please forgive me, Tommy, my brother, is divorced, and he's not handling it too well. I just thought that if he had someone he could talk to, or take out from time to time, he would forget all about her and move on with his life."

Lisa frowned and gently massaged her forehead. "What makes you think I can deliver him from 'evil?' I have to get my own life on track."

A sound distracted Fisher and he said, "Hold on for a minute, Clayton, don't hang up." Fisher looked up to see an individual walking into the office. Lisa could tell that he has placed his hand over the mouthpiece of the phone. She listened intently and realized that it is another civilian for Fisher to recruit. "Ah yes, if you would grab one of those brochures over there that interests you, I'll be with you shortly."

Fisher turned his attention back to Lisa, "Hey, are you still there?"

"Yeah, I'm here," she responded, and by now she was nibbling her nails.

"Sorry about that, this young man keeps coming in, but he can't make up his mind as to what he wants to do. Anyway, listen, I think it would be wonderful if you could stop by before you leave. When do you ship out?"

"I leave in a couple of days."

Fisher pressured, "Like as in two days – a few days – what?"

Lisa sighed loudly, "I have one week left to date."

"Oh shoot," Fisher exclaimed, "That's fantastic! Tommy has about that amount of time left too." He then explained in a calming tone, "Clayton, I know this may sound off the charts, and it is – but I believe that you could really help him. I understand that you are no psychologist, but just your mere presence would give him something to look forward to."

"Sergeant Fisher, who says I'm looking to be tied up with a man or anyone, my last week at home? And I certainly don't have it in me to dress an emotional man's wounds." She shook her head in annoyance, "I'm sorry, but you'll have to recruit another babysitter because I'm not the one."

Disappointed, Fisher responded, "Alright, alright, I guess I did overstep my boundaries. But at least drop by tomorrow, I would love to see ya." Fisher looked up at the young man who entered his office and saw that he was getting antsy. He then turned his conversation back toward Lisa. "Ok, gotta go," he said, and then quickly hung up.

———————

That night, Lisa asked Laura if she could borrow her car the next day. She didn't want to have to explain where she was going and hoped her mother would not probe. Her request was granted and without provocation. A cheerful, but yet curious Lisa, drove to her hometown recruiter's office. She stood delighted to see him – to share her ordeals of training and to show off her toned body. Lisa stood 5'3 and only weighed 102 pounds when she enlisted. Now she weighed 125 lbs. which shows every curve that her new muscles could reveal.

Her arrival at the office was brief as she only lived a couple of miles from Main Street. She remembered so vividly the day she walked into Fisher's office, defeated, insecure, and unsure of her future. But now, things were looking up. Things were looking promising for her. She did not want to be a burden to Laura as Greg has been. Lisa just wanted to make everything as peaceful as she could, because, in her mind, Laura had suffered enough.

Lisa quickly parallel-parked, grabbed her purse and rushed to the pamphlet cluttered door. Fisher stood assisting someone in hopes of recruiting them. He briefly glanced at the door when Lisa snatched it open. Fisher's eyes widened and he tapped the individual lightly on the shoulder and whispered, "Check out these few MOSs – I'll be back in a minute," He then strolled over in Lisa's direction.

"Look at you, girl!" He cleared his throat and then placed his hand over his chest and said, "I mean soldier. Clayton, you have seriously done a complete transformation!" He looked Lisa up and down, smiled, and said, "I need you to be on display around here in this small town. When they see you, they will be breaking their necks to enlist." He looked over his shoulder and whispered to Lisa, "That's that same dude. I don't know what he's waiting on! Shoot, if you ask me, everyone should serve their country for at least two years."

Lisa smiled as she glances around Fisher's body to see the young man. "I totally agree," she said and peeped again. "But the Army ain't for everybody."

They both chuckled. Finally, the young man walked toward the two and gave the brochures back to Fisher. Fisher raised his eyebrows and took the pamphlets, "You still couldn't find anything 'Young Blood?'"

"Nah, I'll be back tomorrow. For sure I'll find something that I might like then."

"Ok, I'll be here," Fisher said and tapped the leaflets in his palm. As soon as the young man walked out, Fisher shot Lisa an annoyed glimpse. "That joker is not trying to join nobody's Army." He then quick-stepped to the door and looked back at Lisa, "Look at him," Fisher said, "He has the most slothful walk. Those drill sergeants will have him for lunch daily, you can believe that!"

Lisa added, "You got that right! I was checking him out." She shook her head. "They will have a good time breathing down his neck as you would say."

Fisher didn't respond. Instead, he stood gazing through the door. He then opened it abruptly, accompanied by a loud greeting and a jovial handshake. "What's up, man!" shouts Fisher. He successively tapped the visitor on the back and hurriedly walked toward Lisa.

"Lisa, this is my brother, Tommy – Tommy, Lisa."

Lisa took a deep breath and extended her hand toward Tommy. He smiled and gently shook her hand. Lisa could not help but notice how handsome Tommy stood. Fisher and his brother laughed and talked, while Lisa stole glances at him, while consecutively viewing Army leaflets. Now and then, Tommy would glance her way and at one point, their eyes did meet. Tommy's physique stood perfectly erect. He was medium build, and about 6'3". His hair was jet black with waves that would make you seasick just gazing upon them. His teeth set perfectly aligned and glistened when he smiled.

Lisa thought, *"What was I thinking? Heck yeah, I could have a ball with him before I leave. I mean what harm could it be?* Lisa placed the leaflets aside and watched the two brothers chat away. Finally, Tommy walked over to Lisa while Fisher stood aloof.

"Hey, ah, Lisa, would you mind joining me for dinner tonight? I know this is quite a spontaneous invitation, and you have the right to decline – I just…

"… sure," Lisa chimed as she stood. Taken aback, Tommy smiled and glanced in Fisher's direction, who smiled and rendered an approving nod. Tommy rubbed his hands together.

"That's great!" And they both said simultaneously, 'Where are we going to…' Their awkwardness ended in a chuckle. Tommy pointed his hand in Lisa's direction and said, "You go first. Is there somewhere that you have in mind?"

"Well, since this is on short notice," she smiled sheepishly and continued, "How about, we ride over to Suffolk for some scrumptious seafood!"

"That sounds good to me!" Tommy beamed.

Lisa walked toward the door and then turned to meet a gawking Tommy. "Let me take my mother's car home, tell her my plans, then I'll call back to the office in about an hour – you can pick me up there – if that's okay?"

Tommy stood with his hands clasped and responded, "Sure, sure, that sounds good to me." Lisa leaned back to catch a view of Fisher, she winked and said, "See you later Sarge!" Fisher walked toward the door and stood solidly beside his brother. "See you soon, little soldier."

Lisa exited the building; she stopped and took a deep breath and scolded, *"I cannot believe I'm doing this! This is so out of character for me. How can I explain my actions, Tommy, dinner and whew, what did I just do! Mama is going to have a fit*

"Girl, have you lost your everlasting mind?" Laura screeched.

"Mom, he's a cool dude! Not to mention he is fine as h…"

Laura snapped, "Uh, watch your mouth." Laura shook her head in disagreement. "I'm flabbergasted, Lisa. You don't even know this guy and you are talking about how fine he is and riding over to Suffolk, VA with him."

Lisa snapped back, "He can't be a serial killer if that's what you are trying to convey, Mom. He's Sergeant Fisher's brother. At first, I was against it. But after I met him, I felt better."

"You felt better huh? So, you're telling me, that after a few hours of chatter, you trust this man enough to ride all the way to Suffolk?"

"Mama, you talk like Suffolk is hours away, it is only half an hour max, depending on traffic." After Lisa made her case, she walked past Laura and into her bedroom. She entered the bathroom, turned on the shower, and stepped inside to allow the warm waters to soothe her nerves. *I wish Mama was not so overly protective of me. Normally, she would be happy for me. But when it comes to men, she almost loses her mind.* She stood for a few more minutes then turned off the shower, dried off, wrapped the towel around her, and left the bathroom. Lisa walked into the family room where Laura and now Nancy sat, neither one saying a word. Lisa stood and looked at Laura and then at Nancy. She finally spoke.

"Dang, y'all would think I'm getting ready to go off to war. Why the gloomy faces?" Lisa then walked over to the sofa and sat beside her mother. She put her hand gently on her shoulder and said, "Mama, it's going to be alright! I'm just going to dinner, that's all. And I will return tonight! You didn't act this sad when I joined the Army, and there are plenty of men there."

Laura turned to face Lisa. "My co-worker just died." Lisa stood and tightened her towel.

"Who?"

Laura looked up at her with tears in her eyes, and responded, "Amelia."

"How, I mean, what happened to her?" Lisa asked.

"Her husband beat her to death," Laura stood and gazed out the window after telling Lisa of Amelia's demise. "I thought everything was going well for her. Although she was a hard person to read. She could be comforting at times and then there were times when she would be short with you. I just can't understand it. The signs were there, we just missed them." Laura abruptly faced Lisa and uttered, "You have to be very careful who you give your heart to, Lisa – very careful."

"Mama," Lisa spoke softly, "Why do you even allow Daddy to come to this house? Are you still involved with him? I mean as much as you have been through with him – he could never dot my door – ever! I'm so sorry about your co-worker, Mrs. Amelia, I really am, but you – you Mama, have made it to safety pretty much. Daddy is out of here. Apparently, Mrs. Amelia chose to stay!"

Laura snapped, "It's not that easy, Lisa! It's not! You're so young and naïve. You think just because you have a little Army training that you can conquer the world!" Laura shook her head from side to side. "When we," Laura pointed to herself and continued through sniffles. "When we give ourselves to a man, we give our hearts, our minds, and every being of our fiber to them. We do this in hopes of getting the same in return. We trust, we love, and we bend over backward for them." Laura sighed, and then looked away and mumbled, "I still love Perry, I do, and I'm praying that he will one day see how much I love him."

Instantaneously, the house phone rang and Lisa jumped to answer. Nancy got up and left the room shaking her head.

"Ok, you ready to copy–my address is Rt. 2 Box 268 US 11 South." Lisa smiled half-heartily and continued her conversation. "Ok, I'll see you in a few." After hanging up, she looked at Laura and remarked, "Tommy is on his way to pick me up, Mama. You can get a chance to meet him." She sighed. "After what I just heard, please allow me to live my life – please."

After Lisa expressed herself, she rushed into her bedroom and donned her favorite faded high-waisted jeans with a white collared shirt. She slipped on her ankle leather boots and short black zippered blazer. The doorbell rang and instantly with a change of heart for an introduction, Lisa rushed to the door, opened it, and closed it behind her just as quickly as she had opened it. Tommy stood with roses in his hands; baffled at Lisa's abrupt exit. Lisa smiled and took the flowers as the two strolled to Tommy's black Lincoln. Laura strutted to the living room window and peered at the couple while Nancy gazed from the guest bedroom. After the couple drove off out of sight, Laura and Nancy appeared from their spying positions. Nancy gazed at her daughter for a long time before she spoke.

"I figured as much–you had not given up on Perry. I sat in this room and listened to you lecture that child. Don't you think you should take your own advice, Laura?"

Laura just stared back at her mother. She continued her gawk and responded, "I really don't know what to do, Mama. Sometimes, when he shows signs of hope," Laura clenched her teeth and continued, "just a glimmer brings me hope, Mama. I'm willing to take that chance with him–I am!"

Nancy pouted her mouth and said, "Even what you heard today about Amelia? That's not going to make you change your mind? I saw you and Perry getting chummy. But I thought it was because Lisa was coming home, now I know. Girl, you better think about that thing. Perry Clayton is not going to change, Laura. It will take an act of God to change him."

Laura turned to face Nancy and responded, "That's exactly what I'm counting on Mama, is for God to change Perry."

CHAPTER IX

Lisa and Tommy grew inseparable. They saw each other every single day that Lisa had left at home. Tommy shared countless hardships in his life. He shared the good times as well, but to Lisa, they were very few and far in between. All Tommy wanted to spew was how badly he had been treated by his ex-wife. Lisa could not help but feel sorry for him. She couldn't understand how a woman could mistreat such a caring man. Lisa loved how he always showered her with flowers and how he opened the car door for her. Tommy really doted on Lisa. There wasn't anything Lisa desired, that Tommy didn't manage to bring to life. He gave her valuable information about how to get settled at her new duty station. For he too, was a soldier. Tommy had the rank of sergeant. That alone flattered Lisa. Each night after their romancing rendezvous, Lisa could not help but fill Laura and Nancy's ears with all they had explored.

It was now Friday, and Lisa was just now allowing Laura and Nancy to meet Mr. Marvelous. She was having such a wonderful time with him that she didn't want any unwanted lectures or vibes from Laura. She was leaving for her new duty station, Fort Campbell Kentucky, the following day. A jubilant Lisa entered the family room clad in dazzling attire. She strolled into the kitchen to get a glass of water. While sipping, she noticed Laura and Nancy watching one of their favorite TV shows. Amid a commercial break, Laura decided to engage Lisa on her date. "I see you are going out again tonight,"

Laura said sarcastically. "So," Laura continued, "Are we ever going to meet this mystery man? All I've ever seen of him is a bouquet of roses and his back. You know you are leaving tomorrow. I sort of thought you would at least spend it with me and your grandma."

Lisa gulped down the last drop of water and reached into her purse. She pulled out a tube of lip gloss and lavishes her lips with it. She puckered and responded to Laura, "This is why I waited until the end of my vacation to introduce Tommy to you. I wanted to enjoy the few little days I had left without any animosity. Tommy will be here within the hour. He is just as eager to meet you guys as you are him."

Nancy stood and said, "Finally! I must say, Lisa, I have to agree with your mother. I got tired of looking at his back and roses. Is that the only flower he knows about? And doesn't he realize that a rose, and especially a red rose symbolizes love?" After Nancy's remark, Laura folded her arms and rolled her eyes.

Lisa tilted her head down and rendered a short wave and said, "You guys, this is not your era! We don't wait a year or two to express our love to one another. Besides, who cares what color the roses are Grandma."

Laura unfolded her arms and then placed them on her hips and responded sharply to Lisa.

"Love–love?" She shook her head and said, "Lisa, you are moving too fast – too fast. You are not giving yourself a chance for Kentucky. There are plenty of people to meet. I thought you would just hang out a couple of days, but you have been seeing him for the past five days – nonstop."

The TV commercial was now off and the regular TV program chimed back on. Laura glanced briefly at the TV but quickly turned her attention back to Lisa. The two women stared at each other for a minute and then the doorbell interrupted their trance. Lisa abruptly looked back at the front door and then turned her attention back toward Laura. "Mama," she said, "please don't ruin this for me." Lisa gestured with her hand slightly upward stepped back and then turned round to answer the door. During this visit, Laura and Nancy stayed put, for they knew the mystery man would soon reveal his frontal appearance. Laura turned the TV's volume down to eavesdrop on Tommy's entrance.

Her heart raced, as she remembered, oh so well, how Perry wooed her. Tommy's voice was deep yet pleasurable to the ears.

Nancy grunted and said, "I see why she kept running out of here every night. Shucks, I can't much blame her." Laura sucks her teeth at Nancy's remark and said,

"Whose side are you on?" Nancy was about to reply but Lisa and Tommy entered the room. Tommy stood, smiling flashing his pearly whites, and armed with two dozen red roses.

He walked over to Laura and said, "Good Evening Mrs. Clayton, it is a pleasure to meet you." He then gives Laura a dozen of roses. Nancy thought to herself, *talking about debonair!*

Tommy quickly scattered her thoughts as he walked toward her. "Good evening, Mrs. Maxwell, it is such a pleasure to meet you." He then gave her the other dozen of roses.

Nancy took them and smiled a broad smile. She then smelt them and said, "Oh my, where did you get these? They smell so wonderful!" Laura smelled hers too and smiled, but half-heartedly.

Tommy answered, "I have my favorite floral shop. It's not local. I don't mind the travel as long as the goods are of great quality."

Lisa stood behind Tommy with her hands clasped in front of her and swayed from side to side. Laura took the flowers and found a vase to put them in. Nancy followed to help. As the two women secured the flowers, Lisa cleared her throat and said, "Mama," Laura looked up after watering the plants. Once eye contact was apparent, Lisa spoke, "Tommy has something he would like to say" Laura never said a word, she then directed her attention toward Tommy, waiting as if he had some type of horrible news to share.

Nervously, Tommy rendered his spiel. "Mrs. Clayton," he then nodded toward Nancy, "Mrs. Maxwell, if I could get your blessings, I would like to drive Lisa to her new duty station."

Laura stiffened her stance and said, "Say what – what do you mean, take her to her new duty station. She already has her plane ticket." Nancy wiped her hands on her clothing and stepped from behind the kitchen counter.

Tommy responded. "Yes, I know – but she can cash it in once she arrives. The military will reimburse her. She can use that cash once she's settled." Lisa interjected, "Mama, please! It will give us more time to be together."

Laura sighed deeply, shook her head, and walked back into the family room. She picked up the remote control and turned the TV off. She then directed her attention back to Tommy and Lisa. Her eyes darted fiercely, from one to the other, and then she said, "Tommy, I've known you of all of five minutes and you want me to let you take my baby girl clean across the United States. I can't stop you," she said while looking at Lisa, "but I am certainly going to try to discourage you. I don't like it."

Nancy stepped up and spoke, "Tommy you seem like a nice young man, but you have to see our side as well." She then spoke softly, "We don't know you."

Tommy walked toward the two women to plead his case again. "I promise you," he said, "I will take good care of Lisa. These past few days have been a joy – why, it's been the happiest I've been in a long, long time. I can assure you; she will be in good hands."

Laura shook her head and sat down on the sofa. She picked up the TV remote and turned the TV back on. Never looking at the couple, she said, "As I said, I can't do anything about it. You are a grown woman now, but I still stand by what I said in the beginning. I don't like it and I totally disagree." Lisa gave Tommy a side glance and nodded toward the door.

Tommy said hurriedly, "Well, it was nice to finally meet you. And I promise I'll take good care of your daughter, Mrs. Clayton." Laura never acknowledged Tommy's remarks, she just held the remote in her hand while staring at the TV. Soon the front door opened, and Lisa and Tommy disappeared into the night.

Laura got up and stormed into the kitchen. She grabbed a wine glass and poured herself a full glass. She sipped and stared at the roses. She gulped and stared at the roses. Her neighbor's dog began to bark, apparently from the opening and closing of car doors or people walking in general. She took her last gulp of wine, put the glass in the sink, and then grabbed the roses from the vase. Nancy turned around abruptly and watched as Laura opened the back door. This time, Laura stepped all the way outside. Nancy stood to follow Laura but stopped at the door and watched her walk in the direction of the barking dog. Nancy's eyes widened as she witnessed Laura toss the roses over at the barking dog. The flowers scattered. Nancy stood in amazement because as the flowers scattered in all different directions, one manages to land on top of the dog's house.

Abruptly, Laura turned to come back inside, she quickly closed her sweater to avoid the evening chill. Before she entered, Nancy hastily grabbed her vase of roses and darted for her bedroom. She gently placed them on her dresser and said to herself, *'She won't throw these good-smelling flowers out. I ain't never had a man to give me any flowers*." She sniffed the flowers again, and again. She stood back and looked at them. Then she whispered a prayer for her granddaughter who was due to leave in less than 24 hours. "Lord help her," Nancy said.

———————

The next morning arrived as quickly as last night's fall. Laura got up, grabbed her robe, and walked to peep into Lisa's room. There she lay sound asleep. It was 5:00 AM, and Laura thought she'd get up earlier to prepare for Lisa's departure. She stood in the doorway of Lisa's room, reminiscing on how just ten years ago, Lisa was just a little girl, all sweet and innocent and always so caring about her mother's needs. Now her baby is all grown up and about to embark on a huge adventure. *Who am I to stop her?* Laura thought. *I just wish she would slow down and listen to reason. Heck, I wish I had listened to my Mama.* She sighed, a deep heavy sigh as she gazed at Lisa's silhouette lying comfortably in the fetal position. Laura decided to wake Lisa up. She wanted to spend just a little time with her before she and Tommy left for Fort Campbell, Kentucky. She touched Lisa gently on her leg and whispered, "Lisa, wake up." Lisa turns over, and rubs her eyes, for a moment, Laura envisioned 'her baby girl, Lisa,' wiping her eyes and smiling at her mother as she always did when Laura would wake her for school.

Lisa, rubbed her eyes again and frowned, then she asked, "What time is it? Why are you up so early?"

Laura responded softly, "I just wanted to spend a little time with you before you leave."

Lisa sat up, "Mama, I really wish you would not worry about me. I'm going to be fine." Lisa then looked over at the clock. She then reached to turn on the lamp. "Let's talk," Lisa said. "I don't leave until 10:00."

Laura took in a deep breath and said, "I just want you to know that I think Tommy has the potential of being a great guy…but you guys are moving too fast. Other than having you and Greg, I wish I would have listened to my mother. Just watch out for the signs Lisa."

Lisa responded, "What signs Mama? All the man has ever done this past week was treat me like a queen." Lisa shook her head and climbed out of bed to use the restroom.

Laura continued to talk. "Sweetheart, you won't see anything now, because it is too early, but if there is anything there, it will surface." Laura paused for a moment, and then asked, "Lisa, did you hear me?" Lisa didn't answer but continued to take care of her business in the bathroom.

She flushed the toilet, washed her hands, and returned to the bed. She pulled up the covers to shut out the cold. She then gazed at Laura and said, "Mama, how is it that you've seen the signs that Daddy had to show, but yet he is allowed to come back into this house. If he were to flip out on you, Grandma is too old to help you. Greg is in jail, and I won't be here. There will be no one to help you. I'm having fun," she said as she hit the bed with her hand. "So please tell me what signs am I to look for – I'm all ears."

Laura drew in another deep breath and replied. "Watch his mood, pay attention if he angers easily. Don't allow him to isolate you, Lisa. Watch his behavior around your friends, check out if he's excessively jealous. Watch and see if he likes to humiliate you in public. These are just a few, and they may seem like nothing at first, but trust me when I tell you, if he is an abusive person… it will get worse." Laura looked at Lisa, who seemingly thought her speech was a joke. Laura could understand why Lisa would feel this way but felt compelled to inform her daughter in hopes of her not having to live life with an abusive man as she has had to do.

"Lisa, I saw a red flag in Tommy, and I've only met him for five minutes."

Lisa responded, "Mom, really? You expect me to believe that? What waving banner have you witnessed?"

Laura responded, "He's controlling."

"Controlling!" Lisa shouted. "How can you say that Mama?"

"I find it absurd, that he wants to go out of his way to drive you to Ft. Campbell. Why can't he meet you there later – give you a chance to get there and get settled in?" Laura shook her head and said, "That move baffled me."

Lisa angrily said, "Mama, we are not getting anywhere with this conversation. I don't want to leave here, mad at you. So, please, let me do me, and you do you, with Daddy and his barrage of red flags that you are still ignoring." After Lisa's reply, she turned out the lamp and rolled over to catch more sleep before she was due to leave on her journey.

CHAPTER X

Daylight showed brightly through Lisa's bedroom window. She rose from her comfortable position and peered out the window. To her surprise, Tommy sat in his car. She quickly glanced at the clock. He was two hours early. Lisa donned her robe and stepped briskly to the front door. She finally got Tommy's attention with continuous waves of her hand. He got out of the car to greet her.

"Hey, Sweetheart," he said as he gently placed both hands on her arms.

A shivering Lisa, asked, "What are you doing here so early, Tommy?

"I just thought I would come by early that's all, you know to help you pack or to load up the car." Tommy peeped around Lisa to gauge the inside of the home and said, "I didn't want to wake your mom or grandmother, that's why I didn't ring the doorbell."

Lisa glanced over her back and decided to allow Tommy to enter. He turned sideways to pass Lisa and entered the home. A nervous Lisa offered coffee, but Tommy declined. She then made enough for herself and poured a cup. She sipped and said, "So, does your early arrival mean we are leaving early?" She sipped again after asking Tommy.

He answered, "I would like to leave early if we could. What do you think your folk would say about us leaving sooner than expected?"

"I wouldn't like it one bit!" Laura stated surprising the couple with her presence. She continued, "You are just going to leave like that, and not say a word, Lisa?" Laura then walked passed Tommy who made himself comfortable sitting at the table in the kitchen nook.

After she passes, he stood, "Mrs. Clayton," Tommy stated nervously, "We – I mean, I had no intention of us leaving without saying goodbye. I was hoping to beat the traffic, that's all." Laura rolled her eyes at Tommy, who after witnessing her reaction, quickly sat back down.

Lisa stood leaning against the counter, still sipping on her coffee. She smiled at Laura, and said, "Now, Mom, you know I don't roll like that. I was going to make sure we said our goodbyes before we left." She finished her coffee, put the cup in the sink, turned toward Tommy, and spoke confidently to Laura, "Like I told you this morning, I'm not leaving until 10:00." Lisa then looked at her mother, who stood proud of Lisa's remark.

Laura responded, "Ok, that's more like it. Let me get Mom up, so we can spend what time we have together before you leave." Laura then directed her attention to Tommy and said, "If you don't mind, I would like for you to leave so that we can spend this time alone with Lisa."

Tommy gazed at Lisa for an interjection, but the expression she rendered guided him to his next move. "Ok," Tommy answered. He then rose from his seat and replied. "I'll be back at 9:30?"

Laura responded, "No, you come back at 10:00." Again, Tommy looked Lisa in the eyes as if seeking a disproval of Laura's stance, but Lisa tightened her lips and nodded her head toward the door, telling Tommy in silence to leave.

———————————

Lisa and Tommy were finally on their way to Ft. Campbell. Lisa grabbed the road map and anxiously tried to map out the destination. "How long is the drive to Ft. Campbell, Tommy?"

"I don't know, maybe about 12 hours or so, depends on how many times we stop."

Lisa replied, "Wow, that's a long drive, but I'm up to it. The only time I think I would need to stop would be just to use the restroom and to stretch."

Tommy didn't answer, he just continued to drive. Soon, Lisa, bored of looking at the map, tossed it on the back seat and settled to take a nap. She drifted in and out of sleep. Sometimes the music startled her if she was in a night of deep sleep or the slowing down of the vehicle would disturb her.

After about four hours into the drive, Lisa finally decided to wake up to take in the surroundings. She noticed interstate signs that read, Ft. Jackson take the next exit. She frowned as if to remember the directions of the road map. She thought, *maybe he's taking a different route – a shorter route.* But when she thought about it, they were never supposed to be in South Carolina period! They should have been traveling West and toward, Tennessee. Abruptly, Lisa reached for the road map as Tommy veered into the lane to exit toward Ft. Jackson. She perused the map frantically and then hysterically asked Tommy if he had gotten lost and why were they heading to Ft. Jackson, South Carolina.

Tommy pulled up to a gas station to refill. But before he exited the car, he told Lisa that he had to go to Ft. Jackson, where he was stationed to pick up his paycheck. He rambled on about some sort of backpay that the military owed him for re-enlisting. Lisa stood horrified for she was due to sign in at Fort Campbell by midnight that very night. She realized that the unexplained detour Tommy took would certainly jeopardize her arrival and that she would be noted as AWOL (Absence Without Leave).

Tommy got out of the vehicle, but Lisa frantically called out to him, "Tommy!" She screamed. "Do you realize what you have done? Why would you take this route? I have to sign in tonight, Tommy – tonight!" But her pleas fell on death's ears as Tommy continued walking into the gas station, and never acknowledging Lisa's cries. He filled up the gas tank and quickly hopped back into the vehicle. Lisa frantically searched the road map for an alternate route that would get them to Ft. Campbell before midnight which was approximately eighteen hours away! She began to sweat, placed her hands over her mouth, and then pleaded with Tommy.

"Tommy," she said wearily, "This is my career, what are you doing? We can never make it to Ft. Campbell now – never! I'm going to be AWOL."

Tommy pulled out toward the highway and smiled at Lisa as he drove to the road toward the interstate. Finally, he said, "You're alright, we can call once we get to the hotel. They will extend your time; I'll talk with them."

Now Lisa stood really baffled, for she did not know they were going to a hotel. She thought about what Laura tried to explain to her. Laura's voice echoed into Lisa's ears, "I see red flags, Lisa. He is controlling, Lisa! Watch his behavior…" Lisa quickly placed her hands over her ears. She began to cry inside while trying to show strength. *This can't be happening. I'm sure he has good reasoning for changing routes other than picking up a check.* She then asked, "Tommy, couldn't you have picked up your check in your own time?" Tommy didn't answer. Lisa then asked, "Why didn't you tell me we would be stopping at a hotel?"

Tommy hit the steering wheel with his fist. He then made this reply, "Shut up! All you women do is complain! I told you I had to get my check – alright? And I'm not driving 18 hours to get you to Ft. Campbell." He then glanced over at Lisa who by now was tuning him out. She had her head turned toward her window, gazing at the cars passing them by. She witnessed, other couples laughing during their travels, while others were viewing a road map and pointing to nearby exits.

Lisa realized she was in grave trouble, simply because she had witnessed this type of erratic behavior from her dad toward her mom. Laura's voice seemed to steal her thoughts and rang out louder than before. "Don't let him isolate you, Lisa." Immediately, Lisa thought that isolation was soon to be a part of her future. She became angry at herself for not listening. She thought about the safety net at home and how pleasant it was to be there when she first arrived from Basic. Occasionally, she glanced in Tommy's direction. His once soft demeanor was now hardened. Lisa began to plan her steps once they arrive at the hotel. *I'll call Mom, once we are there, to let her know what has happened.* But then she thought. *I don't want to worry her. I'll just wait until I make it to Ft. Campbell…that is if I make it.*

———————

Tommy opened the door to the hotel room and tossed his bags on the bed. Meanwhile, Lisa struggled to bring her luggage inside. She placed them close to the door. Tommy went to use the restroom. While he was there, Lisa quickly stepped to the phone to call home. But before she could finish dialing the number, Tommy abruptly emerged and hung up the phone. He then turned Lisa to face him. He gazed into her eyes. She turned her head. He reached for her chin and redirects her face toward his. He finally spoke, "What's wrong with you – you think you're too good for me – is that it?"

Lisa never answered, she just lifted her eyes toward the ceiling. Tommy then pushed her onto the bed. He began to unzip his pants. A frightened Lisa squirmed toward the head of the bed to avoid what she believed to be Tommy's erroneous gratification.

He smiled wickedly and crawled on the bed toward her, but Lisa shuffled briefly to the other side and jumped off. She headed for the door, but Tommy seized her by the arm and snatched her around to face him. He grimaced and said, "Let's try this again." He pushed Lisa hard onto the bed and before she could move he was on top of her. She screamed, scratched, and fought with every inch of her being. But she was no match for the 6'3" 200lb man. The more Lisa fought; the angrier Tommy got. She remembered her mother telling her when she was very young that if a man tried to hurt her and she could not get away, "Hit him as hard as you can in his balls! He will leave you alone then!"

"Owwww!" Tommy bellowed, followed by a painful grunt. He rolled over off Lisa, holding himself between his legs. He rolled and grunted. An astonished Lisa jumped to her feet and scrambled to the hotel door to get out. But as she fumbled with the doorknob a familiar clicking sound rang out in her ear. Tommy had emerged from his crippling pain and got his gun and cocked it. "Make another move and I'll kill ya!"

Lisa put her hands up, never looking back. She stepped backward, very slowly. From her peripheral vision, she could see Tommy's anguish, and she didn't care, not one bit. Her side glance caught the barrel of the gun and Tommy's swaying it to gesture the direction he wanted her to follow. She sat down at the small round table, near the door. Tommy gazed at her. Lisa bit her bottom lip and mumbled, "You never meant to take me to Ft. Campbell, did you?"

"Shut up!" Tommy raved. "Hell naw, I wasn't taking you to Ft. Campbell, you and your fat tail mama were more stupid and gullible than I thought you were."

"So, you drove me all the way out here to rape me?" Lisa countered.

Tommy grumbled, "Naw, not really – I just got horny after the long drive. Don't flatter yourself. You ain't all that. I got my career to think about too."

After Tommy made his sarcastic remark, it seemed he regained his strength, and he straightened his posture. He sat on the side of the bed and lit a cigarette. Lisa rolled her eyes at him and gazed out the window for a moment. She then got up, got her suitcase and went to take a shower.

After her return, Tommy lay on the bed flipping through channels on the TV. Lisa briefly walked by fully clothed, she sat down at the tiny round table not knowing how things would turn out. All she knew was that she wished she had watched for the signs her mother warned about. And as she reminisced, the signs were there, but she failed to recognize them. Why? Simply because she was too young. But then, she had witnessed them oh so many times before, through her dad. The abrupt anger for no reason, and the quick change in mood.

Lisa sat, gazing out the window, and nervously shaking her foot. She wished she were on the other side of that window, anywhere but in that room with Tommy. She stole a side glance of him lying on the bed. To her amazement, he lay asleep with his mouth wide open. She crept to the bathroom to put on her shoes and grab her suitcase. As she was about to leave she caught a glimpse of her face and neck in the mirror. *What has this devil done to me – now I have to report to duty late and with these bruises on my face and neck.*

Angrily, Lisa tiptoed to the nightstand far from the side of the bed where Tommy laid deep in slumber. She thought, *Should I do it or just go?* She reached into the nightstand drawer and pulled out the gun that once stopped her dead in her tracks. She pointed it at Tommy, bit her lip, and cocked it. The clicking sound quickly disturbed his sleep. He opened his eyes but did not seem to be the least worried. He flashed a wicked smile and made a motion to move.

Lisa quickly stepped back with the gun still pointed and said, "Get up and take me to the nearest airport."

But Tommy still showed he was not troubled. He looked at Lisa and said, "You call yourself a soldier." He then reached under the pillow and pulled out the magazine clip. He looked at Lisa and shook his head with a hideous chuckle. "Did you actually think I was going to whip your behind and leave a loaded gun within your reach?" He shook his head again, "You are dumber than I thought you were."

Instantaneously, Lisa's arms dropped. Tommy got up and snatched the gun. He stepped back while placing it back into the nightstand. Lisa flopped back into the chair and gazed out the window, that by now showed flickers of car lights coming and going.

Tommy patted the bed and said, "You can always come over here. I won't bite. I promise – well maybe just a nibble."

Lisa rolled her eyes and remarked angrily, "No thank you!"

The next morning, a weary Lisa remained dressed in the clothes she put on the night before. Her bags were still sitting by the door. Tommy, with a cigarette hanging out of his mouth hurriedly threw his belongings back into his luggage. He took a moment to draw on his cigarette and then picked up his things and walked out the door. Lisa quickly followed and the two got into the car, neither saying a word.

Lisa reached for the map, but Tommy discouraged her from doing so. "You don't need that," he said, after puffing on his cigarette. Lisa threw it in the back seat and folded her arms tightly. Tommy glanced toward her and said, "Look, I'm sorry about last night, this whole ordeal just got out of hand. The money that you have from the airline tickets will get you where you need to be. Fort Jackson is my permanent duty station." He looked over at Lisa, but she continues to stare in the opposite direction. "I guess I should have told you I was stationed here."

"Yep," Lisa retorted, "you should have told me a lot of things." She finally looked straight ahead and witnessed signs pointing toward the airport. Shortly, Lisa found herself, getting out of Tommy's car with bags in tow. She slammed the car door. He flashed that annoyed incredulous grin and sped away.

Lisa hustled into the airport to schedule her flight to Fort Campbell. Disappointment grazed her face as the concierge explained the flight's schedule. Lisa got her tickets and boarding pass. After checking her luggage, she sought desperately for a place to eat. She was famished! Last night left her hungry, in dismay, and embarrassed.

After Lisa devoured her meal she found someplace to sit, where she could hopefully gather her nerves. Her thoughts raced back about the trip down to South Carolina and what had transpired during and afterward. *How could I have been so dumb?* She thought. Lisa continued to allow her thoughts to take their place in her mind, so much so, that she put her head down on the counter of the waiting area and dozed off to sleep.

It seemed as if Lisa had slept for hours when she was awakened by one of the custodian women.

"Miss? Are you ok?"

Lisa awoke, squinting. Startled, she rambled around for her purse and carry-on bag. "Oh no," Lisa squealed. "I gotta get to my gate! I cannot miss this flight!" She looked up at the woman who stood holding Lisa's boarding pass that had fallen during her nervous scuffle.

The woman spoke as she gave Lisa her document. "You have not missed your plane. It doesn't leave until another three hours. I'm just concerned about those bruises on your face and neck. I spotted you when you walked over to my area." The woman then stooped to look Lisa in her eyes and whispered, "Who did this to you, Honey?" Immediately, flashbacks of Tommy's brutal antics and abuse surfaced. The woman spoke again, "Can I get you something?" Lisa didn't answer. She bit her bottom lip and motioned to get up and go toward her gate, but the custodian continued to pressure her. And as Lisa stood, the lady stood. She stepped in front of Lisa. "Are you safe?" Lisa stares at the woman. She is thinking, *why is she so concerned about me? Ok, I'm bruised, but what is it to her?* Just then the custodian's co-worker strode over. She too looked at Lisa and then said to her co-worker, "You found another one?" The lady looked slightly in her co-worker's direction and nodded. By now, Lisa was wondering what in the world is going on. *Who do they think I am?* she thought.

The co-worker spoke to Lisa. "Ma'am, you should just go on and tell Miss Ruby here what's going on. And by the looks of it, you done gone and let some man just beat you pure silly. We see this all the time." The co-worker shook her head and walked off sweeping up crumbs from the floor.

Ruby gave Lisa a concerned motherly look and said, "You in the service ain't you?" Lisa nodded 'yes.' By now tears were streaming.

Ruby continued, "Who did this to you? You a pretty girl, why you let some man do you like this?"

Lisa answered, "I – I didn't know he was like that."

Ruby stepped to a nearby table and got a napkin. She dabbed at Lisa's tears, and then she said, "Honey, I see this all the time. At first, I thought you were some runaway, but when I saw your boarding pass say, Ft. Campbell, I figured you were in the military." After Ruby finished dabbing Lisa's tears away. She stepped back and said, "Listen, it was not your fault. Don't go blaming yourself. You just have to watch out for those kinds of men. Trust me, I know. I didn't mean to pry into your business, but I could not help but notice that you had been in a terrible fight. Just pay attention the next time. OK?"

Lisa nodded. She then spoke in a soft voice, "Thanks, Miss…"

The custodian interrupted and replied, "… Ruby, Miss Ruby is what they call me."

Ruby then grabbed her mop and began mopping where her co-worker had swept. Lisa could not help but notice Ruby's hand. Her ring finger was much shorter than the rest of her fingers. Lisa cleared her throat and asked, "Miss Ruby?" Ruby looked toward Lisa, and answers, "Yes?"

"What happened to your finger?" Lisa simultaneously pointed as she asked.

Ruby answers, "Oh girl, this injury is old, but one I will never forget." Ruby then gave Lisa a proud look and responded, "I lost it in a fight with my ex-husband." Ruby looked at her finger and sort of touched it as if to extend the loss. "We were fighting something fierce that night. After I realized I was not going to win, I tried to run out the door to jump into the car. Once I got that car door open, my sleeve somehow got caught on the door handle. As I tried to free myself – here he comes bolting out the door trying to get at me. And just as I manage to get loose, he slams that darn car door with all his might. I could not move my hand in time. It took my finger clean off." Lisa grimaced at Ruby's description. Ruby looked at Lisa and continued, "You know, my mama used to always tell me never to fight a man because you will not win." Ruby shook her head and moved the mop over the same spot she mopped earlier.

Lisa watched as Ruby mopped and then she told her all about her ordeal with Tommy. Ruby would stop mopping momentarily and react with "What?" And "Mmph, Mmph, Mmph." After Lisa finished sharing her torment she waited for some much-needed advice from Ruby. For she now had witnessed another battered woman, just like her mom, and grandmother too. Lisa stood certain that she did not want to have anything else to do with Tommy and made a pact with Ruby that the relationship had ended.

Ruby responded to Lisa's declaration. "Well young lady, it was so nice talking with you. I best be moving on. This is not a small airport. I'm glad to hear that you will not be messing with that fighting fool anymore. Just remember what I told you… Watch out for the signs and leave them alone because if they hit you just one time, they will do it again. You got lucky this time." Ruby then pointed in the direction of the restrooms. "Go on in there and freshen yourself up a bit. Keep your head up, everything is going to be alright."

Lisa smiled, gathered her things, and did as Ruby directed. She hurriedly stepped toward the bathroom. But before entering she glanced over her shoulder to see if she could see Miss Ruby, but Ruby had faded in with others who littered the airport with luggage, travelers, and beeping cars. Lisa stepped inside and went straight to the mirror. She was astonished at what she witnessed gazing back at her.

She gently touched her face and noticed finger markings on her neck. Tears flowed quickly, as did the presence of other travelers. Lisa rushed to turn on the water to splash on her face, intentionally mingling the water with her tears. She grabbed a paper towel to dab her face dry. She had no idea she looked as horrible as she did. *No wonder Miss Ruby kept asking me all sorts of questions. I did not look this bad last night. What am I going to tell the people at Ft. Campbell?*

Lisa combed her hair and fixed herself up the best that she could. Somberly, she walked out and walked toward her gate. Onlookers peered, and at onset, Lisa put her head down to avoid the stares. She then heard a familiar voice.

You take care now!" Lisa abruptly turned in the direction of the voice to see Ruby and her co-worker standing off in a distance, bidding her goodbye. Lisa waved back and smiled feebly, and then she remembered Ruby's advice – 'You keep your head up; everything is going to be alright.'

At that moment, Lisa tilted her head high. She smiled and walked briskly toward her gate. One more hurdle to face – and that is to hope Ft. Campbell doesn't punish her too severely for being AWOL. Lisa continued her stride, and when the travelers stared, she stared back. Finally, she reached her gate, and before she realized it, she was boarding the plane.

Lisa settled in her seat. She thought about Ruby and her gut-wrenching story. She thought about Laura and Nancy and how they were probably worried sick by now. But she had a remedy – one that would suffice once she got situated. *I'll let one call do for all.* She thought. Lisa soon drifted off to sleep. A much-needed rest stood at hand. This 20-year-old has endured too much agony in 48 hours than most.

CHAPTER XI

At first, the welcome center at Ft. Campbell did not want to believe Lisa's story, for they hear these sorts of tales all of the time. But Lisa stood adamant about her complaint and offered her hometown recruiter's number to validate her failure to report on time. The NCO took her up on her offer. In a rendition of Lisa's story, Fisher stood appalled and offered numerous apologies.

So, that part of her life was behind her. But what the welcome center NCO (Non-Commissioned Officer) did not understand was why Lisa did not want to press charges against her abuser. Lisa's answer remedied the fact that she never wanted to face or have anything to do with Tommy again.

She just wanted to get on with her life. She received treatment for her wounds and was dismissed to her new duty station. *Finally!* Lisa thought. *I made it!* Once she signed in and got a key to her room in the barracks, she hurriedly ran downstairs to use the payphone to call home. Of course, Laura and Nancy were worried but at the same time elated to hear from her and to know she was now safe.

However, Laura tried to persuade Lisa to press charges against Tommy, but Lisa rebutted, "Mama, I don't ever want to see him again – ever! I wish I would have listened; I swear I do. But there is no need of crying over spilled milk. It's over, and now I'm here getting ready to embark on a brand-new career."

Laura responded, "Well, what did that recruiter have to say about his crazy brother?"

"He begged me not to turn him in," Lisa replied.

Laura responded, "So, say no more – now I truly understand why you are not charging him." Laura paused and then continued, "Lisa, he's just going to do it to another young lady – you can help to stop that."

Lisa breathed deeply, "Mama, I pray that doesn't happen. Right now, I just don't feel like going to court and trials – I just want to get started with my new job here at Ft. Campbell. I'm so happy that they did not charge me with AWOL. I desire to forget about the last 72 hours and prepare for my future."

"Now that I know you are doing okay, I'm happy for you. Take care of yourself and call us to let us know how you are doing. We were worried sick!"

Lisa chuckled, "OK, and I will!"

Lisa explored all avenues of Ft. Campbell, literally! During her survey, she located the Top Six Club located on the base. The dining facility was a must and let's not forget, the very place where she would spend a lot of time working and perfecting her MOS. The World War II wooden buildings remained and offered a resident community for soldiers to perform their duties.

Remarkably, Lisa enjoyed her new surroundings, the historical buildings, the climate, and making new friends. Soldiers who had been stationed there for a while did not mind showing her around, and for the most part, Lisa liked everyone she met. Most of the soldiers, especially the male soldiers, were quite friendly. Many but, not all of the females were obliging. Simply because of Lisa being the new girl on the block, which stole the attention that other female soldiers once received.

Nonetheless, Lisa was not about to allow simple jealousy to ruin her or distract her from what she came to do. She stood destined to pursue her new career, meet new friends and explore the world, and nothing was going to get in her way – nothing – at least that is what she believed.

———————————

Lisa had been at Ft. Campbell now for a couple of months. Her explorations soon paid off and she found herself cozying up to some pretty defined individuals, who competed for her attention. However, Lisa stood cautious to ensure she was not impeding on anyone else's territory.

A loud knock startled a drowsy Lisa as she lay relaxing after a long week at work She jumped to open the door. To her surprise, stood a handsome young man. She had seen him several times before because he lived in the same barracks and down the hall – just a few doors from her room.

"Hi, I'm Giles," the visitor stated. "And I wanted to know if you were interested in riding to the mall with me later this evening."

Shocked and excited, Lisa answered, "Sure!" And then she asked. "What time are we leaving?"

Giles smiled and replied, "Just as soon as you get dressed." He noticed while speaking that Lisa was donned in her PJs.

She briefly looked down at herself, laughed, and remarked, "Yeah, I guess I do need to put on some clothes, huh?"

Giles smiled again, and replied, "That would be a good idea. You don't want to get frostbite."

This outing was one of many. Giles and Lisa seemed inseparable. He worked in the same building as she did and was always available to give her a ride back to the barracks. There, they would take in a movie or go to concerts in Nashville. Lisa was so excited about her new relationship, and as far as she could see, he had not shown any signs that her mother, grandmother, or even Ruby conveyed.

Soon, Lisa invited Giles to come home with her. She didn't have a car yet and thought it would be a good idea if he would show up just so her family could meet him. At first, Giles was reluctant about going, but Lisa continued to implore. She finally wore down his resistance, and off to North Carolina, they went.

During the drive, Lisa could not help but steal a glance or two at Giles. To her, he was so handsome. He stood just a little taller than she. His hair was that of a fine grade. It was naturally curly and black. His skin was light, with a slight hint of tan. He was witty, very smart and Lisa liked him a lot. She turned her gaze from him and gaped out the car window, thinking about how Laura and Nancy would perceive him. The only negative component that Lisa observed about Giles was that he consumed alcohol – but shoot, what soldier didn't drink? And that would be her defense if she had to use any at all.

Soon, and after a long 12-hour drive, Lisa and Giles made it to her small town, Ahoskie. Giles was taken aback and teased Lisa with every step they took as they stumbled over tree limbs and small potholes in the spotted driveway. Stumbling and almost falling, Giles managed to say, "You didn't tell me you lived in the boonies!" After his remark, he almost fell. He cursed, and Lisa laughed and replied, "Ooopps, watch your step!" She could only see glimpses of his face from her home's interior lighting. Suddenly, the front porch light popped on and Laura ran outside to meet them.

"Here, let me help you with your stuff." Lisa refused, "Oh no Mom, we got it. Go back inside, we are right behind you!"

Giles whispered upon Laura's retreat, "No we're not, I can't see a thing. Come back, come back!"

Lisa laughed and whispered back at Giles, "Boy shut up, it ain't that bad!"

He continued to step as if walking on hot coals to avoid the unseen sunken grounds. Laura stood at the door, grasping at her robe to ward off the chill. As soon as they made it to the door, Giles seemed to be out of breath, and Laura asked, "Are you ok?"

He answered, "Yes, Ma'am," and then glanced back as if he were trying to locate their path to the front door, but his glance was met with the thick darkness.

"Y'all come on in," said Laura. She then glanced over her shoulder and called for Nancy. "Mom, they are here!" Nancy rushed out of her room at the speed you would expect for a seventy-seven-year-old woman. Lisa met her in mid-stride and they hugged and greeted each other warmly. Laura got her hugs and welcomes in and then divvied out the sleeping arrangements. Lisa showed Giles where he was to sleep and she hurriedly took her belongings to her room.

The visit was short but amicable. Lisa could feel the scrutiny Laura and Nancy seemingly exuded. But nothing negative was emitted during their visit and Lisa was happy about that. Although from time to time she witnessed Giles' uneasiness, he remained with a red solo cup of his favorite beverage, gin, and juice.

The ride back to Ft. Campbell was partly quiet and then sometimes there were outbursts of laughter as Giles found various adjectives describing Lisa's birthplace. For the most part, Lisa felt the visit and Giles' demeanor were acceptable – but what she couldn't parse was Laura and Nanny's stance, for neither woman chose to speak their mind before she left. Lisa took it as a good sign.

The long drive soon ended, and Lisa found herself back at Ft. Campbell. She sighed a feeling of relief and spoke softly while looking out at the sights of the base. "I really like this place. There is so much excitement!"

Giles looked over at Lisa as he pulled into the parking lot of their barracks. He then remarked, "Girl, anywhere is more enjoyable than where we just came from." He put the car in park and continued, "And the fact is, you don't look like you would live in such a small town like that. The way you carry yourself, I thought you lived farther north."

Lisa shot back, "Let's not get so high and mighty. I've yet to witness your location, Mr. Giles."

Giles grabbed his bag from the trunk and retorted, "Let's just say this, it has sidewalks, and a paved driveway and that's all I got to say. Besides, you will get a chance to see it soon."

Lisa frowned and grabbed her bag and they both walked hurriedly to the barracks. Once inside, Lisa decided to stop by the payphone to call her mother. She'd promise to do so as soon as they arrived. Giles nodded at her gesture and continued up the three flights of stairs.

"Mama!" Lisa chimed. "We are back in beautiful Kentucky!"

"Wow, y'all made good time! Giles must be a speedster!"

Lisa took in a deep breath at Laura's remark – partly because she called her boyfriend by name. She then asked, "So, Mama, neither you nor Grandma said anything about Giles, and there were plenty of moments to do so as he is a late sleeper."

"Lisa, I didn't want to say anything while you were here. I didn't want to cause any anger on his part, and he does something to you as Tommy did."

Lisa sighed, "You think he is like Tommy?"

"He drinks an awful lot, Lisa. I can't believe you didn't pick up on that." Laura said cautiously.

"I knew you were going to say something about his drinking. All soldiers do that. I've even drank with them when we all go out or just sit around in the barracks. It's nothing wrong with that."

"Lisa, it is when you drink all day, and every day. When he did get up, the first thing I saw him with was that red solo cup."

"And Mama, you don't know what was in it. You're just finding something wrong, that's all."

Laura sustained her response, "Lisa, nobody drinks orange juice all day long. I even noticed his mood; his eyes were glassy, and he became silent and distant." She then sighed and said, "Look, I'm glad you guys made it back safely. Just keep your eyes open. I love you."

"I love you too," Lisa said quickly, and then hung up. She picked up her bag and murmured while walking up the stairs. *"I knew she would find something wrong. No matter who I allow Mama to meet, apparently she is not going to like him."* Lisa finally made it up to the third floor. She passed Giles' room; his door was open. As she passed, she witnessed a female soldier inside, she brushed it off and continued toward her room.

Shortly, after arriving in her room, there was a soft knock on the door. *Mmph,* she thought, *that doesn't sound like Giles' knock.* Curiously, she quickly stepped and opened the door. There stood a beautiful dark-skinned girl. In fact, it was the same girl whom Lisa witnessed in Giles' room earlier. Lisa remembered seeing her in their unit, for she admired the girl's graceful run when they ran during PT (Physical Training). *'She runs like a deer!'* Lisa would say to herself each time they ran. The girl continued to stand in the doorway, and finally, Lisa stopped daydreaming about her elegance and invited her inside. The soldier was still in uniform. Lisa remembered that too. She hardly ever saw her in civilian clothes. Lisa stood excited upon the visit for she was hoping to finally get close to some of the females there – especially the ones she noted to be kind.

"Hi, Drew!" Lisa greeted cheerfully.

Drew greeted softly, "Hi Clayton," She then looked around and noticed unpacked clothing strewn around Lisa's bed. She then asked, "Did you go home?"

Picking up clothes and putting them away, Lisa answers cheerfully, "I sure did!" She then stopped putting away clothing for a moment and looked at Drew and asked, "Where are you from Drew?"

Drew answered, "Chicago."

"Wow, that sounds, interesting. I heard it was a very nice place! I hope to see it one day," Lisa went back to opening drawers and placing her clothes inside. She felt like she was the starter of the conversations such as it was. However, she still stood amazed that Drew stopped by and hoped it would turn into something very friendly. "So," Lisa opened, "what have you been up to?"

"Just chilling during this four-day weekend, that's all." Drew then took in a deep breath and said, "Look, Clayton, I came by here to ask you a question."

"Okay, what is it?" Lisa responded.

"Are you and Giles seeing one another?"

Taken aback, Lisa answered, "Yeah – yes we are. In fact, I took him home to meet my family this weekend." After Lisa's remark, she could see tears well in Drew's eyes. Lisa put down her clothes and walked closer to Drew.

"Are you okay?" Lisa asked.

"Yeah, I got what I came here for. I just wanted to warn you though. Giles is a fighter."

"A fighter?"

"Yes, he likes to beat women."

Lisa stepped back and put her hand over her chest. "How do you know this, Drew?"

Drew answered, "He has hit me on several occasions. I didn't have to do anything either; he would just punch or slap me at will. He was my boyfriend until a few moments ago. I noticed he wasn't here all weekend, and when I asked the CQ (Charge of Quarters) where he was he acted as if he didn't know. So, once I saw his door open I questioned where he'd been. He started getting angry and I left and thought I'd come to speak with you."

Lisa flopped on her bed baffled at the news. Drew continued.

"I'm telling you; he will hit you – especially when he gets angry. So be careful."

After Drew's remark, there came a knock on the door, and then it opened. Giles quietly stepped in. He looked at Drew and she put her head down and made her way to the door. She stopped in front of Giles, they briefly looked at each other, and then she left the room.

Giles closed the door and asked, "What was that all about?"

A shocked Lisa sat quietly, she then looked up at Giles and said, "Can we talk about this tomorrow? I'm really tired and want to get ready for PT and work in the morning."

Giles stared for a moment and then quietly stepped out of Lisa's room. She marched briefly behind him to lock the door. As she locked it, she could hear Giles yelling down the barrack's corridor, "Drew! Hey Drew! Wait Up!"

CHAPTER XII

A few weeks had passed since Giles' exposure. Lisa sought transportation from other soldiers to get back and forth to work. She and Giles stood cordial, but that's as far as it went. Lisa found herself going to the dining facility alone. She'd glance around for Giles, but he was never there. She began to wonder if Drew was serious or if she was just jealous of the relationship.

Nonetheless, the separation period had almost taken its toll on Lisa. She had discovered that her feelings were more serious than she had anticipated. And although her information was second-hand, she can't forget that she had not experienced any of Giles' hostility. She hadn't witnessed any signs either.

Lisa had found herself in a precarious situation. What if there were some truth to what Drew had said? What if her mother's observations pan out to be something hideous? Lisa pondered those indications but believed she could be the one to change Giles, even if it were true. After all, he'd been nothing but nice to her. He went home with her and made sure she got to where she needed to be. I'm going to make sure that Mama and the rest see Giles as a nice person – that they are reading him all wrong.

As it would be, Lisa Clayton had discovered that her heart was all in. She looked at Giles when he was not looking. If she heard his deep, raspy voice in the hollow hallway, her heart skipped a beat. She was in love with him, and there was nothing that anyone could say or do to change that. The sneers and whispers took their toll on Lisa. But she was destined to stand strong. She ensured that she would keep her head held high. Keep herself up and wait for Giles to come back to her. At least, that is what she hoped for.

One quiet Friday evening, Lisa decided to go to the phone booth to chat with family for a while. Laura explained Greg's whereabouts and Perry's ins and outs. Nancy had fallen ill and the somber list goes on and on. After much dialog about the family's mishaps, Lisa decided to end the call. She crept back to her room, flopped down on her bunk, and turned on the TV. Suddenly, that familiar knock pierced her ears, and she was eager to greet the caller.

There stood Giles in her doorway. Lisa's heart fluttered leaving her no room for ambiguous emotions. Giles recognized her mood and knew he was forgiven before asking.

"Can I come in?"

Lisa stepped aside and replied, "Sure, sure."

He walked in and turned around just as she was closing the door. He looked at her and said, "I've missed you."

"I've missed you too," Lisa responded quietly.

Giles rubbed his hands together and asked, "So, wanna go to the Top Six tonight?"

Lisa jumped at the chance, "Yeah! Just let me freshen up a bit and I'll knock on your door."

Giles smiled and nodded then attempted to exit the room. He stopped and turned to face Lisa. "I'm glad you said yes." With that, he opened the door and left.

———————————————

The music reverberated as the couple drove into its parking lot. 'Planet Rock,' one of Lisa's favorites, seared the air with its bass and rapping lyrics. A hearty Lisa could not wait to enter the club; her dancing skills stood to be of renowned quality. As soon as they entered the club, and found a table, she abruptly pulled Giles to the floor. Not only was Lisa an extraordinary dancer – she was a vigorous one as well. None of her moves stood subtle. Her body would not allow it as she could not contain the energy that the music delivered. She and Giles danced for three disco songs straight. By now, he was ready to sit down. But not Lisa. One would have thought she had been caged like a wild animal. But that was just how she was. She was energetic, spontaneous, and a happy person who despised negativity – no matter in what form it presented itself.

As soon as Giles walked off the floor, someone else grabbed Lisa's arm for a chance to disco, and she obliged. While the dancing partner whirled her around she caught a glimpse of Giles, sitting at the bar ordering drinks. Giles then walked over to their table while bobbing his head to the music. After another two dances, Lisa rendered a nod to her partner and left the dance floor. She grabbed a napkin from the table and wipe sweat from her forehead. Giles smiled and offered her a cold drink. Lisa looked at the glass and asked, "What's in it?"

"Nothing," Giles answered. "Just Pepsi, that's all."

"Good," she said. "I don't feel like getting lit tonight – I just want to have fun!" She sipped on her drink while dancing lightly in place and admiring other partygoers who showed off their dancing moves.

Giles glanced at Lisa while she stood eyeing the partygoers. He sipped his drink, never taking his eyes off her. Lisa finally sat after the DJ interrupted with an introduction to the next song. Screaming and jumping to their feet, the partygoers joined others on the floor. Lisa took a huge gulp of her soda and put it down. She got up quickly as she knew her rising would signal that she wanted to dance. But Giles continued to sit sipping and soon it wasn't long before another soldier walked up to her and asked her to dance. She bolted at the request.

After hours of dancing and singing, Giles was ready to go back to the barracks, and he couldn't gather their belongings fast enough. Lisa laughed all the way to the car expressing the enjoyment she experienced. "This is really a nice club! And the DJ was awesome too!"

"Yep, he's got a reputation for himself, that's for sure," Giles uttered.

Once Giles and Lisa arrived back at the barracks, he asked if he could come in for a while and Lisa permitted him to do so. He closed the door behind him, and they enjoyed one another's company until the next morning.

———————————

The next weekend, Giles purchased some tickets to a concert. Lisa stood elated to go.

"Don't take too much time dressing up as I want to leave early to get a good parking space and find our seats," Giles mentioned to Lisa a few hours before the concert.

Lisa chimed, "I won't! I'll be ready!"

As Giles had forewarned her, he knocked on Lisa's door at the exact time he had relayed to her.

"Come in – it's unlocked," she shouted.

Giles entered with just his pants on. "Girl, what are you doing?"

Lisa lying on the bed with her hair in rollers answered, "I'm blow drying my hair; what does it look like I'm doing!"

Giles looked at his watch and snapped, "I want to leave in 15 minutes. At this rate, you are not going to make it."

"Yes I will," she said with a chuckle. She then smiled at Giles seductively and reached to grab the belt loop in his pants. She pulled him closer to her and said, "Come here with your hairy chest." Giles stepped closer not because he wanted to but because of the pressure felt from Lisa's tug. Lisa then playfully took the blow dryer and lightly tapped it on Giles' stomach, and said, "I'll be…"

Before she could finish her statement, she felt dazed. When she got her thoughts together to find out what just happened, she discovered Giles standing over her with his fist clenched. She tried to get up, but he hit her so hard that it scattered her curlers across the room. By now, Lisa realized what had transpired and she rose to the occasion.

She leaped from the bed and with all of her body weight, charged at Giles. He fell to the floor. Lisa stumbled over him to gain access to her wall locker. While trying to keep her eyes on him, she simultaneously grabbed a cast iron frying pan and hit Giles as hard as she could as he attempted to get up. As he was in motion to fall, Lisa hit him again. A bewildered Giles shook off the blows and as Lisa lifted the frying pan for another strike, Giles lunged at her legs throwing her off-balance. Lisa let out a howl as her body collided with the floor. Giles began to return his striking blows.

By now, and as the fighting ensued, the CQ heard the commotion and ran toward Lisa's room. Other soldiers followed, and soon the brawl was broken up. Giles hurled obscenities toward Lisa as the CQ struggled to get him out of the room. By now other soldiers became aware and stood outside of Lisa's room trying to catch a glimpse.

Finally, the CQ was able to contain Giles. He ushered him to his desk to write an incident report. Lisa could hear people in the hallway, talking about her and Giles' relationship. She shrugged it off the best that she could and wearily began to straighten up her room. She was so despondent that she did not realize her door was still open, allowing everyone privy to what occurred minutes earlier. She walked somberly to the door looking down to avoid stepping on numerous objects that became projectiles during the scuffle. As she reached for the doorknob to close the door, her eyes met Drew's. Not saying a word, Drew stood, exhibiting an older black eye injury. Lisa remained speechless; for now, she had witnessed the first sign in a mighty way.

The two women stared, both with teary eyes. Lisa finally attempted to speak, but as her lips parted, Drew turned and walked away. Another female soldier met Drew and put her arm around her as they walked toward Drew's room. Lisa closed her door, and for the first time in her entire life, she understood how her mother felt about her dad. She slumped on her bed and tried to figure out what triggered Giles' anger. *All I did was tickle him with the blow dryer. That's all I did.* Lisa thought.

Lisa figured she knew Giles, but she really did not have a clue. Even though they dated for many months, she really did not know him. Giles had a history, one she was not privy to. Oh, the signs were there. But when you are inside the eye of the tornado, you are experiencing a different atmosphere. It seems to be calm, blistering with sunny skies. Lisa had a lot to learn. Circumstances play a huge role in why abusers hurt others. History plays a huge role, and so does a person's lifestyle. All these things can be easily hidden if you are on the inside looking out. But there is a pattern to all of this madness. You just have to have the experience, the willpower, and the agility to seek it out.

CHAPTER XIII

A couple of weeks had gone by and Lisa has now found herself alone again. The pain of not seeing Giles as her boyfriend, cut her deeply. But she could not afford to get into scuffles with him. If she did, he may hurt her and bad. The difficulty of her situation was that she had to face him daily. He would always stand outside his door watching as other soldiers come and go. It was almost as if he was scoping out someone in particular.

As Lisa quickly made her way passed Giles' door, he would just stare – and then sometimes he would speak accompanied with a smirky grin. She kept walking, never acknowledging his presence. All she wanted was to get to her destination without any fuss, or conflict.

One day, while at work, Lisa spoke with one of the NCOICs in charge of her workstation. She asked, "What can you tell me about Jonathan?"

"Who, Giles?"

"Yeah," Lisa continued, "What can you tell me about him?"

The sergeant smiled, and then responded, "Giles is a character, to say the least. He thinks he is God's gift to women. But he ain't nothing but a true player." He paused and then looked up at Lisa from his desk.

"I didn't think a young woman like you would get mixed up with a joker like that."

"What do you mean," Lisa asked.

"Giles is an angry young man. And for what, we haven't figured that out yet. He's been in the Army for about four years and cannot seem to get promoted." He looked at Lisa's collar and said, "Prime example," he said with an upward gesture of his hand, as he continued. "Take you for example – here you are just getting in the unit good, and you are already an E-4, the rank as Giles, and how long have you been in the Army?"

Lisa answered, "Almost two years."

"See," the sergeant answered with a smile. "You are fast-tracking! Which is a good thing." He then surveyed his surroundings and said, "Giles can't stand that about you. And when you find someone who is painfully jealous of you–you got nothing but trouble. I suggest you leave him right where you found him because he is not going to be in this man's Army too much longer."

Lisa bit her bottom lip and then asked, "Did you hear what happened in the barracks a while ago?"

The sergeant shook his head, "Yeah, I heard – and that's all the more reason that you need to leave him alone. He ain't no good, I'm telling you – no good."

Lisa gave a half-smile and walked back to her desk. She thought long and hard about what the Sergeant conveyed to her. *How could I not see this about Giles? Boy, was Mama right about him. She is going to be happy about it too. Talking about egg on my face! Whew!*

Lisa brought her attention back to her work. It was almost time to get off. She wanted to make sure she finished her assigned task, the transaction register. Soon, the call for clean-up echoed in the workplace and Lisa hurriedly tidied up her desk and then did her afternoon duties handed down to her by the NCOIC. Soldiers around her were tackling their duties as well. Lisa looked around while emptying the trash. She needed a ride back to the barracks but didn't know who to ask. She walked over to another soldier's desk to gather the trash from his trash can.

As she was stooping to place another clean bag inside the can, she decided to ask the soldier if she could catch a ride with him back to the barracks.

He answered while never looking up and said, "Sure, just give me a minute and I'll be leaving shortly."

"Thanks, Mason, I really do appreciate it."

Busy with his work, Mason smiled and continued with, "I'll meet you out on the stoop out front."

"Okay," Lisa shouted back as she scurried to collect the remaining trash. She grabbed her hat and headed out the door. On her way out, she saw Giles and Drew seemingly all chummy with one another. With a shake of her head, she whispered to herself, *whew, you can have him"* Lisa tossed the trash into the dumpster.

As she walked back to the building to sit on the front stoop, Mason walked out the door. He stretched and yawned and asked, "Are you ready to go?"

Lisa chirped, "Yep!"

The two walked toward Mason's black car. It was old but clean. Mason had a fetish for older cars. Lisa learned that much about him on the ride back to the barracks. Mason took an abrupt detour, looked at Lisa, and said, "I gotta stop at the Shoppette." He pulled into a parking space and quickly jumped out of the car to go inside. Almost in mid-stride, Mason stopped and jogged back to the car. He peered into the window and asked, "My bad; do you need or want anything?" Lisa nodded indicating

'No." She watched as Mason ran into the store. He was a handsome young man – tall with almond skin.

However, he looked a little old to only be a Spec Five which was one rank above hers. Lisa quickly observed that most of her military colleagues were straight out of high school with no college courses to help initiate fast promotions. She also noticed that a lot of them, like Mason, waited about five years after completing high school to join the military. Hence the fact that Mason appeared older, she assumed he fell into that category. Nonetheless, he's always been nothing but nice to her.

His room in the barracks was on the other side of the stair rail and adjacent to Giles' room. Lisa remembers how Mason always rendered a nod as she scurried by to gain access to the stairs. He kept to himself a lot. She had never seen him at the Top Six Club but would always see him standing in the doorway of his room while other soldiers walked here and there trying to get out on the town.

Finally, Mason arrived back at the car with clanking beer bottles in tow. "Are you sure you don't want anything?" He asked as he looked at her with dreamy eyes.

Lisa answered, "Yeah, I'm sure. Just as soon as we get to the barracks, I'm going straight to the dining facility."

Mason smiled, while starting the engine of his car and said, "I hear ya – I think I might go there myself." Lisa didn't know what to think at that moment. Although she was as lonely as could be, she was not going to ask Mason to eat dinner with her. She decided that she was going to stay away from dating and concentrate more on learning her MOS.

Soon Mason approached the barracks parking lot. He parked his car away from others. Lisa watched as he backed into the parking space. He caught a glimpse of her observation and remarked, "This here is what you call combat parking – you don't even know when you will have to leave in a hurry." Lisa laughed at his remark and grabbed her hat, he grabbed his beer and they got out of the vehicle. While walking toward the barracks, Lisa caught a glimpse of Giles' red car pulling into the parking lot. She noticed Drew sitting proudly in the front seat.

Mason chuckled and said, "For the life of me, I never understood what you saw in that dude." He watched as the car passed them. "And Drew either! She is so nice and quiet."

Lisa took a deep breath, "I don't know either. But I'm sure I've learned my lesson. I can't answer for Drew, but he won't be darkening my door anymore."

Mason stopped dead in his tracks and immediately looked at Lisa. *Oh boy, there goes those dreamy eyes again!* thought Lisa.

Mason remarked, "Are you sure about that?" He then pointed at Giles' car with Drew inside as they parked. He then said, "I don't know what that joker got, but he must have something mighty special. He has women all over the place. And no matter how badly he treats them, they seem to not get enough of him."

Mason chuckled again, then gently touched Lisa's arm as if to guide her back in the direction that they were walking. He started humming a familiar song, "I can't get enough of that funky stuff – I tried – I tried!" He then looked at Lisa and laughed and said, "That's you huh, Clayton?"

Lisa chuckles back, "What?"

"Oh, you know what I'm talking about." Mason then bit his bottom lip and repeated the lyrics while playing an invisible instrument. "I can't get enough of that funky stuff – I said woe, woe, woe, woe, woe, woe, YEAH!" Mason looked at Lisa with a bright smile, but Lisa was not smiling. She was thinking and hoping with everything inside of her that Mason's surreal taunting would never come to pass. She had to be strong, no matter where her heart tried to lead her.

Mason continued his charade of singing. *"Lottie, Dottie da, hey, hey, hey – lottie, dottie, da.."* Abruptly and without warning, he turned to Lisa and asked, "Hey would you like any company at the dining facility?" He asked while pretending to beat an imaginary drum.

Lisa hesitated for a brief moment, and answered, "Sure, but I'm hungry now and don't feel like changing out of this uniform."

Mason made a hissing sound with his mouth and said, "You ain't said nothing but a word. I wasn't changing either!" They took a quick left turn and walked toward the dining facility. Occasionally, Lisa would steal a glance or two at Mason. She admired how he handled himself, his style, charisma, and charm. She also liked the fact that she has never seen him with another female soldier.

She smiled as he told the dining facility cook what he wanted on his plate. And when it was her turn she said, "I'm having the same thing."

A few months had passed now, and Lisa and Mason had become an item, at least to others in the barracks. But it was not the truth as far as she and Mason were concerned. All they did was go to and from work, watch TV, and play cards. Others saw it differently, simply because they were always together. And as innocent as their relationship was to them, just living in the barracks opts for nosey people putting everyone together once you are seen in each other's company more than once.

But nosey neighbors did not bother Mason and Lisa. They just simply enjoyed one another's company, plain and simple. One evening, while watching TV in Mason's room, Lisa mentioned to him that she was going home to purchase a car.

Mason interjected, "Good for you – you deserve it."

Lisa smiled, "Yeah, I think it's about time. I wanted to save enough for a down payment to keep my monthly notes to a minimum."

"I don't blame you on that. Have you thought about what kind you wanted?"

"Yeah, I'm looking at a Buick Regal. I like the body style."

Mason nodded in agreement and replied, "OK, OK – yeah those are nice."

He then asked, "What color?"

"Black," Lisa replied.

After a long pause, Mason said, "So, I guess that will be the end of the road to our friendship huh?"

Lisa tilted her head back and said, "Why would you say that?"

"Oh, nothing," he sighed and said, "Well, I have been giving you a ride every day, and taking you where you needed to go – I just thought…"

Lisa got up and walked over toward Mason, she sat beside him and interrupted his sentence…

"… I will still be your friend. You have been good to me and have not expected anything in return. I'm so grateful for that. When I come back with my new ride, you can ride with me to work."

Mason smiled and started to ask Lisa something but changed his mind. She felt he had something to say and then asked, "What were you about to say?"

He smiled and looked at her for a moment and said, "Do you mind if I come with you?"

Lisa paused. Mason speaks again, "If it would be a problem, I understand. You go on home and handle your business."

She smiled and felt relieved to not expose him to her mother who, she is almost positive, would shoot him down, simply because of his poise. To her, Mason was a desirable man. He was thoughtful, a hard worker, and witty. Lisa loved the relationship that she and Mason shared, and she did not want anyone else's opinion. Things were finally looking up for her and she is enjoying life as it should be, peaceful and unrestricted.

CHAPTER XIV

A few weeks after Lisa and Mason's conversation about her purchasing a new car, it soon came to fruition. She pulled up in the parking lot of the barracks late on a Saturday afternoon. Heads turned as she drove in pursuit of a parking space. She spotted Mason's car and decided to park near his. To her surprise, he was sitting inside his car, smoking a cigarette. He smiled as she attempted to combat park.

She looked over at him and smiled, turned the engine off, and said, "You like?"

Flicking ashes from his cigarette, he opened his car door and got out. He gave the car a look over, smiled, and said, "This is nice! I like; yes indeed, I like it. No one will be able to tell you a thing now!"

Lisa chimed, "Good! I'm glad. I didn't think you would like it because it is a newer car and I know you are into older models."

"No – no," Mason interjected, and then pointed at his chest, "You ain't buying it for me – this is for you, and it is beautiful just like you."

Lisa blushed and said, "Oh thank you, Mason! I was hoping you would like it."

Mason smiled and flashed those dreamy eyes at Lisa. Soon, she found herself surrounded by other soldiers hanging out in the parking lot oohing and awing at her new car.

"Yo Clayton, this you?" a soldier shouted as he walked closer to gaze upon the vehicle.

"Yep!" she stated cheerfully

The soldier replied, "Girl, this is nice!" After his remark, he briefly acknowledged Mason and turned to walk back to the others who had rendered their congratulatory remarks.

Lisa took a deep breath and stated to Mason, "Well, everyone seems to like it!" She looked down at the tires. "I'm going to put some new rims on it."

Mason answered, "Nah, you are going to mess it up, don't get any rims."

"Too late! I've already queried about some and hopefully, they can put them on next week."

"When did you have time to do all of that?" Mason asked.

"I called a place off 41A while I was at home. I go in on Monday after work to look at some on display. I'll decide then."

Mason shrugged his shoulders, tossed his cigarette butt on the ground, and put it out with his foot. "If that's what you want? It's your money."

Lisa grabbed him by the arm and led him toward the barracks. "I have something to tell you," she murmured coyly.

Mason stood happy to finally have all of Lisa's attention. He smiled and said, "What's that?"

"I'm planning on moving out of the barracks soon."

He stopped and looked at Lisa and replied, "When – I mean why?"

"I want my own place. I've already talked with the First Sergeant, and he said no problem. I've never liked staying in the barracks – too many nosey people. There is no privacy either!"

"Aren't you full of surprises today!"

"Yep!" Lisa chimed, "I sure am! But moving off post won't be for a little while. I have to check places out and I want to be close to work."

Lisa and Mason continued to walk back to the barracks arm in arm. and for the first time, she felt as if she was in control of her life. She was taking slower steps with Mason. She wanted to watch his every move, find out more about him. I guess one could say, she was interested in taking their relationship to a whole new level and if that premonition materialized, she was determined that it would be on her terms.

Once they entered the barracks, Lisa stopped at the phone booth to call home to inform Laura that she had made it in safely. After her brief conversation, she hurried up the stairs to put her things away and spend more time with Mason. As she approached the landing, she heard Giles' voice. She thought, *Oh, I was hoping he would be somewhere sleeping or drunk, anywhere but standing in his doorway!"*

Giles' gently reached out and touched Lisa's arm as she passed his door. She stopped, looked down at her arm, and he removed his hand. He then spoke, "I heard you got a new car."

"Yep," Lisa said and started to walk away, but Giles grabbed her by the arm again and said,

"When am I going to get a ride."

Lisa snatched her arm away from him. By now Mason stepped out of his room as he could hear bits and pieces of the conversation.

"Never!" She snapped and snatched her arm away again and strutted toward her room, but Giles was not through, so he followed her.

"Giles!" Mason called out.

Giles stopped and turned slowly around to face Mason. Lisa kept on walking as fast as she could. By the time her door slammed shut, Mason was scolding Giles.

"Leave her alone!"

Giles replied with stretched-out arms, "Oh, you doing her too!"

The CQ recognized that trouble was brewing so he got up from his desk and ushered Giles back inside of his room. Giles continued to yell from his room. "You doing her too, man!"

The CQ managed to get Giles seated on his bunk. He looked up at the CQ, waved his hand at him, and said, "Man, I'm alright – I'm alright."

The CQ nodded and said, "Get some sleep, man. You need to sleep it off."

"Get some sleep," Giles mimicked, "Get some sleep – sleep it off. Yeah, yeah, yeah, I'm alright go on, get out, I'm alright."

The CQ left and closed Giles' door behind him.

Meanwhile, Lisa sat on her bed with tears streaming down her face. That was the first time Giles had spoken to her since their fight. It seemed as if everything she thought she had tucked away for him, had resurfaced. She could hear everything that transpired in the hallway and she actually for a moment felt sorry for him. If only he didn't drink so much. He could be a cool guy to hang out with. She got up to put her clothes away in hopes of getting Giles off her mind. Nothing seemed to work. Finally, and after she'd put away her clothes, she tiptoed down the hall. The CQ saw her, smiled, and spoke. Lisa spoke back. The CQ looked up and was surprised to see Lisa standing in front of Giles' door.

He whispered, "Clayton, whatcha doing?"

Lisa never answered, she just stood in front of Giles' door poised to knock. She knocked.

Giles opened the door; she walked in and remained until Sunday morning.

Lisa promised her mom that she would come home for the New Year, but Giles had other plans. He begged her to go home with him on New Year's Eve. He told her that he wanted her to meet his parents, and when she asked if Drew had met them, he answered boldly, 'No.' She mentioned her going home with Giles to Mason and he thought she was a fool.

"You got to be kidding me! Why are you going home with him Lisa? I don't understand it!"

Lisa tried to persuade Mason that somehow she believed she could help Giles.

"That rascal doesn't want any help – and he darn sure don't want yours." Mason looked down at her with a disgusted look on his face and said, "Who do you think you are anyway? If he gets you in the Midwest, there is no telling what he might do to you."

Lisa put her head down and committed. "I'm going. Besides, I think it is nice of him to ask me to meet his parents."

Mason frowned and became disappointed at Lisa's naivety. He then said, "Lisa, I don't think he has a relationship with his parents."

"But how do you know?"

Mason mocked her, "But how do you know? Look at you – you are SOOO gullible!" He then clasped his hands together, and asked, "When have you ever heard him talking about his folks – huh?"

Mason then stepped toward the door and pointed at the phone on the CQ's desk and continued, "I've been here for about two years, and I have never – never heard the CQ tell him he has a long-distance phone call. It has always been some honey calling for him. Girl, wake up!" He then reached out and touched Lisa on both her shoulders. He looked at her softly, and said,

"Lisa, don't go, I'm begging you, don't do it."

Suddenly, Giles opened his door, stood on the threshold, and gazed right at Lisa, who was standing in Mason's doorway. Lisa didn't realize that Giles' door was open and that he was standing there staring her down. She continued to make her case with Mason, and soon after her last remark, she stepped back and turned towards her room. That is when her eyes met Giles' and with a nod of his head, he summoned for her.

"What was that all about?" he asked as he gently stroked her hair.

"Oh, nothing. I was just asking Mason something about the rims on my car that's all."

"The rims on your car, huh?" Giles spoke dryly.

"Yes," Lisa said confidently and repeated, "The rims on my car." From her peripheral vision, she witnessed Mason standing in his doorway facing the two of them. He stood chewing on a toothpick. He spat the fragments on the floor, shook his head and walked back into his room, and slammed the door.

Giles rendered a smirk toward Mason's room and told Lisa to be ready to leave early in the morning.

Within three days, and while visiting with Giles' family, Lisa's life had turned upside down. The unspeakable happened and she did not know what to do or who to turn to. Giles dropped her off at his parent's home around 6:30 PM on New Year's Eve. He and his dad argued because he brought her to their home and then left. Of course, and without question, Giles returned drunk at 2:30 AM. He jumped on Lisa, who lay awake in a strange home, and he raped her. The next day, they left, heading back toward Ft. Campbell.

Lisa pondered what she had done to deserve such harsh treatment. She felt if she shared what Giles had done to her, no one would believe her. And in that day and time, she was right, no one would believe her. She willingly went to his hometown. And even though his mother put them in separate rooms, Giles crept into her assigned room and raped her. Since their reunion, they had not been intimate, and Lisa saw no need to be on birth control pills for she was abstinent.

Weeks turned into months and soon Lisa found herself throwing up profusely one morning. She was so sick, that she could not perform her duties. To make matters worse, Giles, once again, could be seen wandering through the corridor with Drew. Lisa was so humiliated that she did not want to live. Finally, she went on sick call and as fate would have it, she was pregnant. Another blow to her dreams, her lifestyle, and her life.

A confused now twenty-two-year-old stood at a crossroad not knowing which way to turn. In the early eighties and depending on your performance, the military frowned upon unwed mothers. Lisa now stood facing the possibility of being discharged from the Army. She did not want that–she wanted to stay. She tried to conceal her pregnancy from the company commander and the First Sergeant. She continued to run PT until she was four months pregnant.

Soon the First Sergeant noticed that his avid athlete was not performing as she used to, and he called her into his office.

"What's going on Clayton; talk to me," The First Sergeant said while scanning through files. "This is not like you to fall out of runs." He stopped thumbing through his files and looked up at Lisa. She stood crying. It was on the tip of her tongue to tell TOP (First Sergeant) what had happened to her. As she stood, she remembers his many lectures about cohabitating, as he would put it, in the barracks. She discerned that he would not believe her, as he had witnessed her and Giles' on-off relationship. To Lisa, at this point, it was like trying to explain to someone why you aren't muddy when you stand dripping in it.

"Are you alright?" Top asked.

Lisa continued to stand staring straight ahead and crying.

"No, I'm not alright."

"Well, what is it? Talk to me?"

Every time the words *Talk to me* fell from Top's lips; Lisa wanted to tell him what Giles had done to her. But then again, she also wanted and needed his sympathy.

"I'm pregnant, Top," Lisa stammered.

"What?" The First Sergeant screamed.

He shook his head, "Come on Clayton! How in the world could you let this happen?"

Lisa stood, lips trembling; she could hear a voice in her head saying, *just tell him! Tell him!* As Lisa parted her lips to speak, the First Sergeant asked, "Whose is it?" And then he paused and reached for a form on his desk. He then remarked, "You went home with that no-good Giles didn't you?" He waves the leave form frantically in the air.

He then rants, "Yeah, I remember…" he said while wetting his thumb to easily sniff out Lisa's leave form. "Here it is! You went home with him didn't you?"

A weeping Lisa nodded.

The First Sergeant got up from behind his desk and walked past Lisa. He stood at his door and yelled for the company commander. The captain entered and Lisa could hear Top informing the commander about her deteriorating future. The commander soon walked over to Lisa and asked,

"What do you want to do Clayton?"

"I want to stay in, Sir!

"And how are you going to care for your baby and serve in the military too? That will be a tough task. Frankly, I don't see how it can be done. So, I recommend you file for a Chapter Eight."

Standing at the position of attention, Lisa asked, "What is Chapter Eight, Sir?"

"It is like an honorable discharge, only it's for pregnant female soldiers."

"Is there a possibility that I can stay in, I promise I will do whatever it takes to make this right, Sir?"

The commander and the First Sergeant talked for a moment and both decided to allow Lisa to stay in. But he told her, "You will be fully responsible for getting housing, and having someone care for your baby, is that clear soldier?" the commander asked.

"YES SIR!" Lisa shouted, she then saluted the commander and left the First Sergeant's office.

CHAPTER XV

Although Lisa had a newborn on the way, she would still be able to get things done, make something of herself, and stage a life of happiness for herself and her child. She realized that it would not be easy, but at least by staying in the military; she can keep her head above water.

Lisa now realized she was back on track to fulfill her dreams of becoming a successful and productive citizen. During her pregnancy, she ignored Giles' advances. Proudly she'd step passed his room door as he stood gazing at other female soldiers and walked down the stairs and to her own car.

Once she retreated to the barracks, she spent hours filling out documents to prepare for her son's arrival. There was a family care plan packet to file for, a rentals program, and not to mention finding a suitable location for her and her baby to live in.

At times, Lisa found herself overwhelmed, but she pushed through. At some point and with numerous reservations, she finally decided to tell Laura and Nancy that she was pregnant.

"Oh my goodness, Lisa," Laura exclaimed. "How could you? Now you have gone and just thrown everything away, your future, your…"

Lisa interrupts, "…no Mama, everything is not lost. I've made all of the preparations needed and the I'm allowed to stay in the Army."

Laura breathed a sigh of relief and then she asked, "So, who's going to keep the baby for you? I mean, won't you have to get up extra early? That can be a task within itself with everything else that you will have to deal with."

"Mama, I got all of that under control. I'll make it. It will be alright."

Laura paused and then asked, "So, what does Mason have to say about all of this?"

"Mason?" Lisa retorted. And then she thought, she has never told her mother what occurred on that faithful New Years' Eve.

"Mama, the baby is not Mason's."

"Ahhhh, well whose is it then? Lisa don't tell me you just let yourself loose out at Ft. Campbell."

"Come on, Mama, you know me better than that," Lisa responded and then took a deep breath and remarked, "It's Giles' baby."

"What?! Laura screeched. "I thought you stopped seeing him? Lisa what in the world?"

"Mama, I know what you are thinking, and if I were in your shoes, I'd be thinking the same thing. But trust me, it was not consensual."

"Mmph, Mmph, Mmph," Laura grunted, and then she spoke, "Lisa, oh my goodness. What happened? I mean, did he do this to you in the barracks?"

"No," Lisa answered sternly, and then she continued, "It was in his parent's home."

Laura replied, "See, I begged you not to go home with him Lisa, I did. And now he's made things so much harder – so much harder. Have you told your commander?

Again, Lisa answered sternly, "No."

"Why not? Do you know how this is going to look for you, Lisa?"

"Mama, I really don't care! It can't be any worse than it already is!"

Laura fought back tears and offered gently, "If you want me to, and after the baby is born, I can help you out a little. I'm about to retire here shortly and can pitch in by taking the baby just until you find a place to live."

"Are you sure, Mama? That would be such a huge help. That way, I won't have to rush in finding a place to live. I'll pay you too. The Army has a program for dependents. I'll just give you what they give to me – if that's alright?"

"Yeah, sure – that will be fine. I just want you to take care of yourself." Laura paused and then asked, "Lisa, are there any churches there? You should find one. It's time out for the dance halls. You are going to need the Lord to help you through these next few months. Stop depending on those men. They are only after one thing."

A defiant Lisa retorts, "How's Dad, Mama?"

"Are you serious right now?" Laura shot back. 'Your daddy doesn't have anything to do with what I'm trying to tell you – which is something for your own good." Laura's voice rises, and she continues, "Besides, if you care how he is, then call him yourself. But don't patronize me, I'm grown!"

Lisa shifted her weight on the other leg and responded, "I'm just saying – you can always tell me what to do, but you don't follow your own advice. Why is that Mama? Hello? Hello?" Lisa looked at the receiver and mumbled, "She just hung up on me!"

Over the next few months, Lisa continued to sort things out to prepare for her child. She found an affordable four-bedroom trailer off the main drag from the post. The trailer park was well-kept and Lisa could only hope it would be available after the baby was born.

"Only three more months," Lisa whispered while looking in the mirror at her round belly one morning. "Yep, three more months, and I can have this baby and move on with my life." At that moment, Lisa realized she felt awkward about the way she spoke of her unborn child. Was it the way he was conceived – it very well could be. And having to face her rapist daily, did not make matters better for her. There were times when she would pass Giles' door that he had something demeaning to say to her, or he would try to force her to ride with him to work even though she had transportation. Lisa could hardly wait to leave those circumstances.

But leaving the barracks would be the least of her problems. She had to withstand the ridicule and speech bashing she received each day while standing in formation. It was as if the First Sergeant now despised her.

"I want my barracks cleaned!" The First Sergeant shouted one morning in formation. He stood on his toes and sort of reared back and forth. He then looked down at Lisa's platoon. He squinted and remarked. "And if you use my barracks as a hotel, I will deal with you!" He looked in Lisa's direction again, who stood dressed in a light-yellow sundress, because military tunics for pregnant soldiers weren't available at that time. All other soldiers stood clad in their fatigues. The First Sergeant frowned after gazing for a moment at Lisa, and then he chided, "My barracks is not a hotel! Therefore, if you decide to use it as such, you will be looking like Specialist Clayton!" The male soldiers in formation belted with laughter.

"At ease!" shouted the platoon sergeants.

Afterward, the First Sergeant bellowed, "FALL OUT," releasing the soldiers for work duty.

Lisa gazed around and hurriedly tried to find her way out of the maze of soldiers. Some were strutting around mocking TOP's remarks. Others were leaning back holding their stomachs imitating a pregnant woman. Lisa stepped vigorously to her car. It seemed the faster she walked the faster the tears flowed. But she kept moving until she finally reached her car. Other soldiers passed her car, not recognizing she was seated inside. They were laughing and still imitating TOP's remarks. Lisa rolled her eyes and started her car.

"That's alright," she murmured. "Once I have this baby, I'll show all of them who will get the last laugh."

She then put the car in drive and sped out of the parking lot.

Giles continued his taunting and soon it got out of hand. One morning, Lisa strutted briskly toward her room and passed Giles' room to avoid any verbal or physical contact. Once she retrieved her items she started back out for work. While locking her door, she caught a glimpse of Giles standing in his doorway shooting the breeze with the CQ. As she walked in that direction she made sure to gain eye contact with the CQ. He acknowledged her, and she picked up her pace. Giles also acknowledged her approach.

"Where are you going so early? We don't have to be at work until 9:00. Why don't you ride with me today – save some of your gas."

Lisa ignored Giles' comment and continued to walk. As she came parallel to the CQ's desk, she witnessed Mason standing outside of his room, combing his hair with an afro pick.

"Morning Clayton," Mason greeted.

"Good morning, Mason."

In an instant, Giles grabbed Lisa's arm and whirled her around to face him. He drew back his fist and punched her in the face. Out of reflex, Lisa grabbed her jaw and swung on Giles only to land an imminent blow. She missed. She could only do the best she could to ward off Giles' blows. She thought to herself as she fought. *Oh, Mama, I need you! And why doesn't anyone intervene? She grunted and swung.*

Meanwhile, Laura stood at her job terrified because Perry had amped up his tactics. He came to her job trying to see her. She had put out a restraining order on him and he did not like it one bit. She could hear him outside of her classroom door ranting and raving, demanding to see her. Laura's mind began to race. *I can't believe he's here. We have a restraining order, but he just won't leave me alone. He's here, Perry is here. He's at my job, can you freaking believe this man?*

At the barracks, Lisa let out a scream as Giles yanked her around like a puppet. He pulled and gritted his teeth. He was trying to make Lisa go to her knees, but she refused. She finally realized she was no match for him; she screamed to the top of her lungs.

"Please, somebody help me, please!" She grunted, she cried. Her eyes became blurry as she sought out her surroundings seeking help from other soldiers. Her mind flashed back to the evening she witnessed her dad beating her mom.

"Mama!" she wailed.

At Laura's elementary school, things continued to ramp up. Perry demanded to see her. Laura listened intently as she stayed hidden inside her classroom. She was so relieved that her students were at lunch with the teacher's aide. She crouched down and thought about Lisa, and her question, *'How is dad?'* Laura bit her bottom lip as Perry's voice got louder, she listened to see what the principal had to say to Perry.

She could hear the principal saying he wanted to see me just to talk. The principal yelled out to me and advised me not to come into the hallway.

Suddenly Laura heard the principal radio for the SRO (School Resource Officer).

"No, Mr. Clayton, you cannot go in there!"

Laura's classroom phone rang. It sounded louder than most rings. Her heartbeat seemed to match each ring tone's density.

"Stay put Mrs. Clayton!" the principal shouted.

Meanwhile, Lisa continued to struggle with Giles. She heard a familiar voice shout out,

"Lisa, stop squirming!" It was Mason. He had jumped in to pull Giles off her.

The CQ, was on the phone dialing the First Sergeant's office. After he made contact. He joined in to relieve Lisa of her assailant.

Giles was determined to literally pull Lisa to her knees. But as she struggled, her purse got tangled in her arms. Mason was afraid Giles would snatch her to the floor, face down. She could hit her head causing traumatic injury. They continued to scuffle with Giles. The fight moved closer and closer to the stair rail and the two soldiers realized Giles' intent. Giles growled as he dragged Lisa toward the stair rail with the CQ and Mason holding on for dear life.

Giles growled, "All I wanted was for you to ride with me to work. But you think you are too good, huh?"

Giles suddenly made a motion to lift Lisa off her feet. She moaned aimlessly, like a wounded puppy. Mason landed a blow to Giles' head, stunning him, and the two soldiers thrust and punched him anywhere they could. He had the nerve to swing Lisa's body between him and the licks, something the other soldiers had feared. Nonetheless, Mason produced a powerful punch to Giles' abdomen causing him to fold. Lisa managed to escape his grip.

Meanwhile, back at the school, Laura stayed hidden. And Perry stayed, determined to see her. Before Laura realized it, she was on her feet. She cracked open the classroom door. Immediately, the opening of the door caught the principal's attention and he yelled over his shoulder,

"Get back in there Mrs. Clayton!"

But Laura whispered, "I'll see him – I'll see him this one last time."

By then the SRO approached, with his hand placed on his weapon. Perry greeted him and said, "Man, ain't no need for all of this. She is my wife and all I want to do is speak with her, that's all.

"Mr. Clayton, I totally understand, but there is a restraining order on you. You are not supposed to be here. So, I'm going to ask you to leave, and if you don't, I'll have to use force."

The principal stood, stretching his neck and repositioning his clothing.

Laura spoke, "It's alright, I'll see him."

The SRO looked at Laura with grave concern and said, "Are you sure?"

"Yes," Laura gestured with a wave of her hand. "It's alright. I'll see him this one last time."

Perry smirked, and then looked at the SRO and the Principal. He then casts his arms outward and said, "Can't a brother get some privacy?"

The two men stared at Laura; she nodded in agreement with Perry's request. The principal, fidgety, reached in his pants pocket and gave Laura his radio. "Here, take this. If you feel threatened, don't hesitate to push the panic button."

Laura smiled and took the radio. "I won't," she responded softly.

––––––––––

Concurrently, Lisa ran down the stairs as fast as she could. She pushed through the double doors of the building. As soon as she leaped over the few steps and onto the sidewalk, she ran into the First Sergeant and the Company Commander's arms.

TOP shouted, "Clayton, are you alright?"

The commander asked, "Where is Giles?"

Huffing and puffing, an exhausted Lisa pointed toward the barracks and said, "He's upstairs fighting with Mason and the CQ."

The two men looked at each other briefly and said, "We've got that son of a gun now!"

The commander interjected, "Yep, his career is over as far as I'm concerned!"

––––––––––

At the same time, Laura tried to figure out how to rid herself of Perry, once and for all.

"What do you want, Perry? I'm here, so talk and make it snappy, my students are about to finish lunch shortly."

Perry peered around precariously and said, "A restraining order, really? Did you have to do that, Laura?" He snickered and rubbed his chin, then he said, "I mean, are you trying to keep my grandchild away from me too? I want to be able to come around when Lisa brings the baby home. I want to help you – if I could."

Laura sighed, then glanced at her watch. "Look, I don't have much time." She then glanced over her shoulder and saw her students rising from the table in the cafeteria. Before she could turn completely around to face Perry he had stepped in closer to her and grasped her by the neck.

He then snarled, "You darn right you don't have much time!" Gazing around fiercely he tried to find a connecting corridor to drag Laura to. She struggled to look for the panic button on the radio but to no avail could she make contact. Perry tightened his grip around her neck and scowled, "You are going to drop those orders, and you are going to do it now or else!"

Laura was about to speak, but she felt something hard press against her upper back. She realized Perry had brought his gun into the school. Frantically, she pushed each button imaginable on the radio and soon the SRO and the Principal stormed toward the hallway.

Perry had managed to drift the two of them toward another sector of the corridor. And while the SRO and Principal were en route, the SRO caught a view of Perry's back. He motioned with his head to get the principal to stand down. He softly crept up behind Perry and cocked his gun. The clicking of his gun startled Perry, but he did not look back from whence the sound came.

Laura also heard the clicking sound. She shouted to the SRO, "He's got a gun!" She wept while speaking, "He's got a gun in my back! Oh please, Lord have mercy on me!"

"Put it down Mr. Clayton. Let's end this peaceably."

As the SRO spoke he crept closer. He lowered his voice this time so as not to alert Perry of his closeness. "Come on, Mr. Clayton, let's not do this. Don't you want to see your, grandbaby? Huh?"

Perry sniffled and responded, "Man I can't with this freaking restraining order. Tell her to remove it!"

"You know I can't do that. A restraining order is not a life sentence. But if you harm Mrs. Clayton, I can promise you – you will see a life sentence."

Perry sniffled again, and motioned to speak, and CLUNK! The SRO hit Perry on the head with the butt of his gun! Perry dropped to his knees and Laura dashed into her classroom and locked the door. She hid and began to cry uncontrollably. She thanked God for saving her life and continued to cry while praying. Suddenly, the rattling of her doorknob startled her. She became visibly shaken.

"Mrs. Clayton," the principal called out. "It's ok, everything is under control. You can come out now."

A traumatized Laura slowly opened the door and peered out.

The principal reassured her, "It's ok; he's gone now." The principal then looked at Laura through tear-filled eyes and said, "I want you to get your things, and go home – get some rest. I'll see you in a week or so."

Laura nodded and stepped back into the room to retrieve her purse. As she stepped out of her classroom, she was met with chattering students. She abruptly swipes at her tears and put on a fake smile.

"Hey, Mrs. Clayton!" The students shouted.

Laura nodded in their direction and walked away with the principal. As they walked away from the children, Laura could not help but hear their murmurs,

"What's wrong with Mrs. Clayton," a student asked another.

"I don't know, but she looked like she was crying," another student added.

"What for?" another student shouted. The teacher's aide quickly ushered the children into the classroom. And as they entered, she too could not help but wonder what happened to Laura.

CHAPTER XVI

Buzz was in the air about Giles' dishonorable discharge. Many soldiers were happy because of the nasty attitude he possessed. Others stood elated because now they won't have to worry about Lisa being treated worse than a dog and by his hand. And then some continued to make jokes about her and say that she deserved what she got. See, Lisa, as her NCOIC once told her, was a fast tracker. The mediocre soldiers were jealous of her. It would not be long before Lisa would soon embark on making sergeant. Yes, fast-tracking stood in her midst. Now that Giles was gone, nothing could stand in her way. At least that's what she'd hoped.

Late one night, in Lisa's eight months of pregnancy, the CQ's phone thundered through the corridor. The halls were quiet which spawned a much louder ring. Lisa turned in her bed trying to regroup and fall back asleep when she heard a soft tapping at her room door.

"Clayton, Hey Clayton," the voice whispered.

"Yeah? Who is it?"

"It's the CQ – You got a phone call."

Lisa jumped out of bed, donned her robe, and hastened down the hall. As she strolled, the thought of Giles standing in his used-to-be doorway still frightened her. But she soon realized that he was gone and that she did not have to worry about his presence ever again.

However, she became nervous because of the late hour of the caller. *"I hope it is not Mama or Grandma."* she thought.

"Hello?" Lisa answered the phone with a raspy tone.

"Hey, Lisa."

Lisa screeched, "You've got to be freaking kidding me!" She hung the phone up and stormed toward her room. But before she could open the door, the phone rang again. The CQ answered and beckoned for her to come back.

"No!" Lisa shouted. "Tell him to go to hell!"

The CQ laughed and relayed the message. He hung up and the phone rang again.

Lisa could hear the footsteps of the CQ quick-stepping to her door. She opened it before he could knock.

He said, "Look, if you don't talk to this joker, whoever he is, he is not going to stop calling. It's late and that phone is going to wake the whole barracks. Please talk to him."

There was really nothing Lisa could do but answer the phone. The CQ didn't know what to do, because he was new to the unit. So, he had not yet heard of the incidents that Lisa had endured. Lisa angrily snatched the receiver off the desk. "Look!" she shouted. "I don't want to see you or ever talk to you again, do you understand? And if you continue to disturb me I'm going to tell TOP!"

Lisa motioned to hang up the phone, but she could hear him say, "My dad just died."

Lisa slowly placed the phone back to her ear. Giles continued, "He is gone, and I don't want to be alone through this. Would you please come out here to be with me – to go to his funeral with me?"

Lisa replied somberly, "I'm eight and a half months pregnant. I cannot fly way out west, I'm sorry, Giles about your dad. But I am not coming."

Giles began to cry, "Please Lisa, that's all I ask, please come to be with me at daddy's funeral."

"Giles, I've told you that I am not coming so please leave me alone!" Lisa slams the phone down so hard that it let out a faint ringing sound. She reached behind the phone and turned down the volume. She then looked at the CQ and said, "This is what you do after 2200 hours. Make sure you turn down the volume, so it doesn't wake up the entire barracks. That's a pure fool who just called!"

"So, what do I do if he calls again," the soldier asked.

"You will have to answer it. If he asks for me, just hang up. You won't get into any trouble. He will get the message."

Lisa then turned on her heels and waddled back to her room.

———————

A week later, Lisa, Mason, and a couple of other soldiers were en route to the dining facility. They were laughing and playfully rubbing her stomach, asking her what was she going to name the baby. When she was about to answer, she noticed a red car out of her peripheral vision. She paused while placing her hand on the bottom of her stomach. The soldiers insisted on their request not realizing what she was looking at. Suddenly, their attention was disrupted by a familiar slow-talking voice.

"Hey Lisa, yeah, I too would like to know what you are going to name your baby? Please enlighten the fellows. You always did know how to get them all excited. So, tell them – what are you going to name the baby. And whose is it anyway?"

Mason looked in the direction that Lisa's eyes now pierced, and he said, "Ain't this a mother?" He then asked, "Man, you are not supposed to be on post. You better leave, now!" Mason and the others grabbed Lisa by the arm and walked briskly toward the dining facility.

But every step they took, Giles kept pace with his car – cruising alongside them. He then shouts, "I'm going to kill you, Lisa." He nods his head while chewing on a toothpick, "Yep, your days are numbered–next time this week," Giles stuck his hand out the car window emulating a gun, "Pow," he said and pulled the trigger of his make-believe weapon. "You will be history, dead, gone, the end! "He then sped away.

Mason turned to look at Lisa who was now hysterical. "I can't keep living like this! It seems if I take one step – that devil takes two. He's going to kill me; I swear he is!" Crying she shouted, "How did he even get on post? I thought he was put out of the Army!" She began spinning around to gain eye contact with each of her companions, she continues, "What am I going to do? He could pop up at work; he could pop up out of anywhere!"

Lisa cried uncontrollably and Mason tried to soothe her. "Shhhh," he whispered in her ear. He then gently pushed her back to gaze into her eyes. "After we eat, we are going to tell TOP what just happened."

Lisa interrupted with crying and said, "But…"

"…Shhhh," Mason soothed, "Trust me, TOP will take care of it and Giles will be barred off-post permanently."

The next morning, soldiers rose for PT. Lisa decided to wait around in the dayroom before going out to formation. As she sat watching TV, she heard a loud horn blow. Other soldiers heard it too, and they all ran to the window along with Lisa to see what the commotion was about. Soon, laughter dispersed as Giles sat in his red car, parked on the tennis court, which was directly across from the barracks, honking his horn and calling Lisa's name.

One of the soldiers yelled for the CQ, "Yo, man, call TOP! This mother done lost his mind!"

Giles continued to honk his horn and yell, "Do you see what you have done to me? Lisa!" he yelled. "Come out here and help me."

Giles' enemies got a kick out of his performance. They yelled back, "Go the hell home, Giles! Nobody cares!"

Giles yelled back lethargically, "I don't have a home anymore! Lisa got me put out the Army! I sleep in my car now!"

The soldiers murmured amongst one another, "This fool is pathetic."

Others stated, "Man, he's gone – yep, gone, straight off the deep end."

Another interjected, "Well he ain't falling fast enough for me," The soldier then peeped out the third-floor window again to peer at Giles. He laughed, shook his head, and walked out of the dayroom.

Again, Lisa stood humiliated. She began to despise the day she ever saw Giles. And once again, she took on the stares and the insults. In contrast, some were supportive, and she appreciated every kind word and gesture. But Lisa, realized, that Giles' behavior was taking a toll on her. She didn't care how the abuse stopped – she just wanted it to stop. Lisa had to get away, and she had to get away fast or she was going to lose her mind.

That same day, Lisa requested to take leave at home. She wanted to have her baby where she felt safe. She called Laura and she came to pick her up and drove her back to North Carolina. There Lisa could have some peace. She knew in her heart that leaving Ft. Campbell for her maternity leave would be the best thing she could do. Hopefully, she could now have some peace.

In just a couple of weeks of being home, Lisa gave birth to a six-pound five-ounce baby boy. The delivery was a hard one for her. She suffered immense pain because, for some reason, the baby could not travel down the birth canal. Lisa had to endure a

C-section. After she finally laid eyes on the cute bundle of joy, her heart went out to him. She gazed upon his tenderness, his innocence, and wondered if he felt her pain during the nine months she carried him. She whispered as she held him close to her while gently rubbing his forehead. "It's going to be you and me, little man. What shall I name you?" She thought of a couple of names and quickly shook her head. While in deep thought about what to name him, a nurse rapped softly on the door.

"Yes," Lisa answered with a smile, "Come in," she said as she placed the baby back in the bassinette. Lisa put the baby down because she thought the nurse would want to take some vital signs, but that was far from the truth.

"Miss Clayton," the nurse asked, "Have you thought of a name for the baby yet?"

Lisa smiled, and answered, "No, we were just talking about that." Lisa then reached over to the bassinette to massage the baby's arm. She then directed her attention back to the nurse and said, "I'll let you know once I figure it out," she looked over at the baby and said, "Won't we, little fellow?"

The nurse jotted down a note and then asked, "What is the name of the baby's father?" Lisa's smile quickly faded, and she answered, "He doesn't have a daddy."

The nurse thought Lisa's humor was a bit absurd, so she pressed again. "Sure, he has a father," the nurse said while playfully rubbing the baby's feet.

Lisa gritted her teeth and said, "I said he ain't got no daddy."

The nurse responded, "Ma'am, I need to know the name of the baby's father so I can put it on his birth certificate."

But Lisa would not budge. Finally, the nurse left the room shaking her head.

When it was time for Lisa to leave the hospital, she got tickled after reviewing the birth certificate.

BIRTH CERTIFICATE

NAME: Gregory Allen Clayton

MOTHER'S NAME: Lisa M. Clayton

FATHER'S NAME:---

CHAPTER XVII

Due to the complications of delivering little Gregory, Lisa was granted an extra two weeks at home before returning to Ft. Campbell. While at home, neighbors and high school friends stopped by to see Gregory. Some were filled with all sorts of questions, 'So, Lisa when are you going back? And are you taking Gregory back with you?' And the questions kept coming, 'Why did you name him after your brother?'

Lisa found herself answering numerous questions; she would smile and answer or frown and answer. As others continued with their queries, she thought, *Boy these are some nosey folk!* They even asked how much she got paid! After the excitement wore off about the newborn baby… Lisa wanted to ensure all her documents were signed and notarized. For she had found it to be easier to allow Laura to help her out. And as soon as she arrived back at Ft. Campbell, she would put the deposit down on that four-bedroom trailer she had been eyeing for months.

One cool evening in October, Laura entered the den as Lisa sat feeding Gregory.

"He's so adorable, Lisa," Laura said while gazing at little Gregory, who was sucking the bottle so hard it looked as if he would suck the nipple off.

Lisa looked down at her son and agreed delightfully with her mom. "Yes, he is. And I'm going to teach him how to be a good man when he grows up."

"I'm sure you will," Laura added.

After Lisa finished feeding Gregory, she gently picked him up to allow him to burp. She noticed he was turning red. "Oh, oh," she said with a smile. "We know what that means!"

Laura began to fumble through Lisa's baby bag in search of a diaper. But she remembers that they were all in the laundry.

Lisa asked, "Mom, what are you digging for?"

"I was looking for a diaper; he's going to need changing soon."

Lisa frowned, "Mom, when I leave, please step out of the 1950s and put pampers on my son. That way you won't have to wash those stinking dirty diapers – I can't stand those things."

"Lisa," Laura replied. "You will save a lot of money using diapers. And besides, I don't mind washing them. All you have to do is soak them first and then wash them with your regular clothes."

Lisa put Gregory on his stomach across her knees and bounces her legs gently as she massaged his back. "Mama, I don't like them. Besides, you will have enough money to buy all the pampers he needs."

Laura shot back, "Well he doesn't have any now, and we are in need."

"I get paid tomorrow," Lisa added, "I'll go pick up a plethora of pampers before I leave."

Laura sighed and went into the laundry room to wash the soil-soaked diapers.

Lisa laughed, "See, I'm not about to do all of that! No way, no how."

Lisa put Gregory down for his nap and decided to get some fresh air by walking to the mailbox. Once she retrieved the mail, she thumbed through each envelope. She opened the door still looking down at the mail and said, "Look what I just received."

"What is it?" Laura asked.

"A letter from Giles."

"What?" Laura screeched.

"Yep! And I'm throwing it right in the trash." Lisa strolled to the garbage can and toss the mail inside.

As she walked back from the kitchen, Nancy appeared.

"Grandma, how are you feeling?"

"Oh, I'm feeling pretty good. I heard you went to the mailbox. Did I get any mail?"

"Yeah," Lisa answered. "I put it on the table."

Nancy walked over to the table, picked up her mail, and then took a few more steps toward the kitchen and peeped in the trash can. She turned around quickly to look at Lisa and put her hand on her hip and said, "Girl, why did you throw this mail away without opening it?" Nancy bent down to pick it up, she stumbled a little because of a dizzy spell but quickly regrouped. She looked at Lisa and remarked, "You're not going to open it?"

Lisa replied, "Nope."

"Why not?"

"Grandma – because I don't care about nothing he has to say, I don't want to get pulled back into his madness."

"Do you mind if I open it?" Nancy asked.

Lisa extended her hand and said, "No! Help yourself."

Nancy ripped the letter open in a jiffy. She then remarked, "My, My, My!"

"Laura stepped out of the laundry room and peeped over Nancy's shoulder, "What is he talking about Mama, we don't have any ties with him – so what has he got to say for himself."

"Oh, he didn't say anything!"

Lisa began to get angry, "See, why did y'all take that mess out of the trash? I knew he was playing games that's why I did not want to entertain it."

Nancy walked over to Lisa and handed her the envelope. She then walked back to her bedroom. While en route she yelled out, "Go buy that baby some pampers, Miss Know-It-All!"

Lisa watched Nancy sashay down the hall. She peeped in the envelope and found a $100.00 money order. She was broke, and the money could not have come at a better time.

Laura smirked, "We think Mama is back there asleep and she is just eavesdropping her tail off."

Lisa added, "I know, right! But this time, I'm glad she wasn't sleeping. I certainly needed this money." She glanced around for her shoes, grabbed a light jacket, and headed toward the market.

Lisa didn't know what to make out of Giles' unexpected and much-needed support, but she was glad to receive it. She ensured she made good use of the funds until her next pay period. For she did not expect anything else from Giles. Her expectations came to fruition because that was the first and the very last check she received from Johnathan Giles.

CHAPTER XVIII

Lisa's two-month maternity leave quickly came to a close and she found herself back at Ft. Campbell. She was able to make the deposit and the first month's rent for the four-bedroom trailer. She moved in shortly after returning to Ft. Campbell. Now all she had to do was ensure she could keep up with the month's rent plus utilities before Laura would bring little Gregory to her. Things were finally looking up for Lisa, and she realized she was back on track.

Soon after her return, the First Sergeant became adamant about her going to PLC, (Primary Leadership Course) as it was referred to back in the early eighties. This course would imbue her military status, thus catapulting her into the next phase of ranks. Once the course was finished, and Lisa stood before the E-5 Board, she would receive the next rank of Sergeant. 'Sergeant Clayton' sounded wonderful to her ears, and she was determined nothing would get in her way.

One cool September evening, during Labor Day Weekend, Lisa was invited to a promotion party by one of the soldiers in her company. She accepted. At the party, people were really having a marvelous time. They all cherished Sergeant Harris and stood elated about his promotion. People were dancing and singing and partaking in alcohol and marijuana. Lisa thought nothing of the booze and weed as, throughout her tenure, that's what soldiers did. She had indulged in various drinks but never tried weed.

As the night went on, soldiers became merrier as they continued to indulge in the liquid delights amid smoking joints. Someone walked past Lisa and offered a puff from their marijuana joint, but she declined. After much persuasion, Lisa gave in and decided to try it. Because she had no idea what to do, the soldier offered to blow the smoke up Lisa's nose, which she choked on afterward.

Waving her hand to dispel the smoke Lisa stated, "Whew! That's enough for me."

"Oh, come on Lisa!" The soldier chimed while looking around. "Everybody is doing it, come on, try it!"

Lisa took the joint, she tried to smoke it but still did not have a clue as to what she was doing. She coughed and her throat burned. The soldier laughed and said, "There you go! You got it! Here, hit it again!"

Lisa shook her head while still trying to catch her breath. "Never mind," she said between coughs. "That's enough. I don't want anymore!"

The guy laughed and mumbled as he high-stepped away, "More for me then!" He puffed and coughed as he traveled to entertain someone else.

It was getting late, and Lisa soon decided to go back home. Once she arrived, she decided to call home to check on little Gregory. As the phone rang she began to think about her brother. She wondered what he had been up to. The two of them had not seen each other in such a long time, but Lisa still loved him so. That is why she gave her son his name. She had hope that it would bring him closer to her and that they would be a family again.

"Hello?" Laura answers, interrupting Lisa's thoughts.

"Hey, Mama! I just wanted to check in to see how little Gregory was doing."

"Oh, he's just fine! He sleeps through the night now!" Laura beamed.

"Wow, amazing," said Lisa.

Laura continued, "I could not help but think of Greg while rocking little Gregory to sleep. Oh! And before I forget, Gregory stopped by."

"He did?" Lisa chimed.

"Yeah, you know he was in Virginia working but the work has dried up. He wanted to stay here but I can't handle Gregory's coming and going – not with Little Gregory here."

"So, where is he going to go, Mama?" asked Lisa

"I mentioned to him that you have your own place now. I told him to reach out to you."

Lisa sighed and frowned at the same time. She did not know how to handle her older brother because she hasn't seen him in such a long time.

"Lisa, are you there?" Laura called out.

"Yeah, I'm here, Mama." *Dang, just as I was enjoying my freedom*, Lisa thought.

"So, what do you say?" asked Laura, and then she continues, "I think living out there would be great – at least until he could get on his feet."

Lisa breathed deeply and said, "Mama, I don't know. I'm up for promotion and I have to attend PLC before I can get the next rank. I wouldn't be much company for Greg."

Laura sighed and said, "I understand Lisa, but he is your brother, and he desperately needs family right now. I mean, I got your baby, can you at least sacrifice a month or so until he gets on his feet?"

"Alright Mama, you didn't have to go there about keeping Little Gregory. Remember you offered to help, and I'm so thankful. I just wanted to use this free time to prepare me for the promotion that's all." She sighed and then asked, "When is he talking about coming to Kentucky?"

"He told me in about three weeks or less."

"Okay, tell him he can come; by then I will be in PLC. It's an eight-week course, so I will only have five weeks left by the time he arrives."

"That's good, Lisa! I'm proud of you. I realize that you are younger than he is but maybe he could draw from your ambition and want to make something out of his life."

"I sure hope so," Lisa responded. "Because I'm not in the business of babysitting a grown tail man."

"Ok, well you have a nice night, and I will tell Greg to give you a call."

After Laura's comment, the two hung up. Lisa thought *I got a feeling that this visit is going to be an adventure!* She shook her head at the thought and prepared for bed.

———————

Tuesday morning arrived quickly, and it was time to report to PT and then work. The past weekend was a blast. The promotion party held on Labor Day weekend stood to be more fun than Lisa could ever imagine. And then the thought of Greg's visit made things more interesting. Lisa arrived at the PT formation on time. She prepared her mind for some tough calisthenics since they had just come off a four-day weekend. But to her and others' surprise, all soldiers were told to fall out and go to the Orderly Room. There each soldier was told to take a urinalysis test.

"Why do we have to take this test?" Lisa asked another NCO (Non-Commission Officer).

The NCO answered, "Apparently, the Army is cracking down on smoking marijuana." He looked around observing other soldiers who walked into the Orderly Room, and he continued. "Rumor has it, anyone whose urine has THC in it will lose a rank."

Lisa could not help but notice the nervousness in the Sergeant. She began to ask him a question, but he interrupted her and asked, "Say, were you at Harris' party?"

"Yeah, I was – but I don't remember seeing you there," replied Lisa.

"No, I wasn't there, but I heard it was lit."

As the two stood in deep conversation, a voice shouted, "Okay, next two soldiers, I need a male and a female! Come on soldiers let's move, quickly, quickly, quickly!"

After the surprise urinalysis test, everyone was told to report to their duties and wait for a phone call from the company commander. At work, the soldiers tried to keep their minds on their duties, but the phone kept ringing non-stop. The NCOIC, would hang up and call out a soldier's name. And when they answered, he would say, "Report to the Commander's Office."

Soon one of the first soldiers to report walked back into the building dumbfounded. Everyone rushed him to ask what occurred during his visit with the CO (Company Commander).

He answered, "Man, I just got busted!"

"What?" the others shouted.

"For what?" They asked.

"I came up hot on the piss test." He then looked around at everybody and said, "All of you who went to Harris' party are going to get busted too."

Chatter and murmuring grew louder within the workplace. One of the older Vietnam Veterans yelled out, "If you weren't smoking that crap, you don't have anything to worry about it. But if you were, then you can hang it up! This new CO does not play and she's out to set an example.

After the NCOIC made his rationalization. Lisa casually strolled over to his desk and asked. "Serge, what exactly are they looking for in our urine?"

The Sergeant peered up at Lisa and asked, "Were you at that party?"

Lisa puts her head down, "Yes, I was."

"Did you take part in the weed ceremony?"

"Well, I let somebody blow some smoke up my nose."

"Oh," said the Sergeant, "So, you had a shotgun."

"Huh?" Lisa asked.

The Sergeant laughed at Lisa's ignorance and then he said, "They are looking for THC in your urine. Since you just had a shotgun," he gestures with his hand as if to minimize his comment and continued, "meaning, you allowed someone to blow the smoke up your nose after he/she inhaled deeply, then you might not have to worry." He then gave an absolute gaze with a slight tilt of his head, and added, "Then again, it depends on how potent the drug was. So we will see if your name is called."

Immediately, after the Sergeant's remark, the phone rang. It rang so loudly that Lisa could feel her heartbeat. Lisa stood trembling at his desk. He allowed the phone to rest gently on his desk as he looked around the room and then he yelled, "Mason, report to the CO's office!" He hung up the phone, looked at Lisa with a smile, and continued to do his tasks.

As fast as soldiers trickled out – they trickled back in with long cast-down expressions. The phone kept ringing and the NCOIC kept calling out names, "Harris, let's go – report to the CO's office!"

Lisa moseyed to her desk and sat trembling she just knew her name would be next. Each time the phone would ring her heart felt like it would jump out of her body. She decided to whisper a prayer.

"Dear Lord, please don't let them call my name – please don't. I promise I will never touch another joint again if you would spare me this time. In Jesus' Name, Amen."

Soon, the phone stopped ringing. And Lisa could not be any happier. She walked over to the NCOIC's desk and asked, "Are they done calling for everyone?"

He looked up at her from his seat. "Yep," he replied, and then he added, "You are one lucky soldier!" Lisa smiled faintly and walked away. As she went back to her desk, the soldiers who were there looked up at her. Some rolled their eyes at her while others wondered why she did not get called down – especially when they knew she attended the same party.

One of the soldiers walked up to her and asked, "Hey Clayton, weren't you at Harris' party?" She nodded.

"Well, why didn't you get called?"

Lisa shrugged her shoulders and answered, "I don't know."

She abruptly walked away from the soldier and proceeded to do her afternoon chores for it was close to quitting time. As she swept the floor, she could not help but replay in her mind, what the NCOIC said, *"You are one lucky soldier."* And the other soldier's remark, *"Hey weren't you at Harris' party?"* She grabbed the dustpan and swept the trash onto it. She thought to herself, Luck didn't have anything to do with it. It was God Almighty who spared me and my career. *"Thank You, Jesus,"* Lisa whispered. She dumped the trash, gathered her belongings, and headed to her peaceful abode.

———————————

The next day, Lisa received a phone call from Mason.

"Hey, Lisa," said Mason. "I see you didn't get into any trouble from the party."

"No, I didn't, but you have to remember, I didn't smoke an entire joint, Mason, I just got a shotgun."

"No," said Mason. "I beg to differ. I saw you take a puff. And I sort of got a little angry because I wanted you to smoke your first with me, but that's neither here nor there now. That's not the reason I called. I need your help."

"What is it?" Lisa asked. "I'll do the best that I can to help."

"Well, that's good to know because I really need it." Mason sighed and continued, "Listen, I got busted too from that stupid piss test."

"O-Kaaay," said Lisa. "And you can make the rank back, right?"

"No, Lisa, it is not that easy. This was my third time getting into trouble. Our other commander spared me because I was good at my MOS. But this CO we got now is out for blood! She's putting me out of the Army effectively immediately and I don't have no place to go."

Lisa breathed deeply and responded, "So, I guess you want to come here to stay?" She paused and asked, "For how long Mason? My brother is due to come here in another week or so. Neither one of you has a job and I can't foot these bills alone. Besides, Mama is going to bring my baby here soon." She paused and then continued, "I don't know, Mason, this is a bit much."

Mason replied, "I'll apply for unemployment and then I'll get a job. Lisa, I need a place to stay. Top told me I had a couple of days to clear his barracks."

A reluctant Lisa gave in to Mason's woes. Soon, she found herself boarding two house guests and neither man was working. Now, Lisa was two weeks in with PLC. She made a good impression on the TACT Sergeants. So much so, that she was allowed to come home to her trailer for a few hours. She decided not to let Greg and Mason know she was coming home. She wanted to surprise them and hoped they would be out working or doing something productive to help pay the bills.

When she walked into the house, she noticed the two men seated at the kitchen table.

"What are you two up to?" she asked. "I thought y'all would be out working."

Mason looked up and smiled, and so did Greg. "Nah, we are filling out our unemployment paperwork."

Lisa walked over to view the documents but there weren't any to view.

"What paperwork?" shouted Lisa.

Lisa then leaned in a little closer to see what the men were really up to.

"Y'all aren't filling out any paperwork? You are scrubbing the yellow pages and writing down different places of employment, but you aren't trying to get a job!"

Lisa continued to rant and rave about Greg and Mason's deceptiveness. Mason finally threw his pencil down on the table and got up. Lisa watched as he walked over to the sofa and flopped down. She then shifted her wrath to Greg.

"And you, Greg, ought to be ashamed of yourself. You need to work and pay back some of that money Mama and Grandma has loaned you! They can't keep taking care of you!" Lisa then walked over to the stove to heat up some soup to eat before she had to report back to PLC. While at the stove she continues to blast Greg about his inadequacies. Tired of hearing her fuss, Mason soon got up and went outside.

Lisa continued yelling at Greg, "Mama and Grandma need their money and here you are too lazy to work and pay them back. I did not bargain for this at all! You don't want anything, and you can't stand to see anyone else with something!"

Suddenly, CLUNK!!! Lisa stumbled and grabbed her head. Stunned, she stood staggering and faced Greg, who by now was standing above her and breathing hard. His expression said it all and Lisa realized he was mad as hell. She stepped back to put a little distance between them, and she shouted, "I know you didn't just hit me! Are you out of your mind?"

"Yeah, I hit you and will do it again if you say one more word about me not giving Mama any money!"

Lisa shouted back while still holding her head, "Yes I said it!" She bellowed through gritted teeth, "And I will say it again! YOU NEED TO PAY MAMA BACK HER MONEY! YOU OUGHT TO BE ASHAMED OF YOUR SORRY SELF!"

POW! Greg landed a stinging slap on Lisa's face. But this time she retaliated and with much force. The two tussled, hit, scratched, and punched each other. Finally, Greg had had enough and decided to lay Lisa out for good. He drew back his arm and with a mighty blow hit her so hard that she collapsed on the floor. Greg then pounced on her and swung blow after blow. Lisa screamed and squirmed until she was able to pull herself up by grabbing the edge of the sink. She managed to gain access to the stove. Greg continued to lunge after her. She grabbed the hot pot of soup and dashed it into his face. He let out a howl, while fleetingly swiping at the hot residue that streamed down from his face.

Lisa stood watching as he brushed at the hot contents. She gripped the pot tighter, and as Greg charged at her again, she raised the pot to hit him but lost her footing in the slippery liquid, causing her to fall. Greg jumped her again, beating her to a pulp. Lisa screamed so loud, that Mason heard her pleas for help. He rushed through the door and dove into Greg, forcing him to release his grip on Lisa. Lisa scrambled to her feet. She was soaked in her blood and greasy soup. Her uniform looked terrible, and she was due to report back to PLC within an hour.

As Mason and Greg rumbled on the floor, Lisa yelled, "GET OUT! BOTH OF YOU – GET – OUT!"

Both Mason and Greg left – leaving Lisa in a heap of trouble. She walked over to the table and slammed the telephone book shut. She sat exhausted and cried so hard that her eyes became swollen. *I swear* she thought, *the next man who hits me will be pushing up daisies. I'm sick of men beating on me like I'm some dog. I'm just sick of it. And to think, my own brother?* L i s a ' s cries soon turned into sniffles. She glanced at the old clock on the wall and noticed she had thirty minutes to get back to base. She got up and wiped the contents off her uniform as best as she could. Lisa looked in the mirror to comb her hair. She suffered a busted lip and a swollen right eye. I can't go back to PLC like this – I just can't. Warm tears begin to trickle down her cheeks stinging each laceration. I can't she murmured. I can't go back there looking like this. She dampened the washcloth and dabbed at her now swollen bloody lip.

Too exhausted to drive back to base, Lisa sat at the kitchen table where Mason and Greg once plotted. She peered at the clock again, and noticed, she had only ten minutes to get back to base. I'm already late, she thought. I'm just going to sit here until I get myself together. If they put me out of the academy, then so be it. I'll try again.

———————————

Lisa found herself driving back to base. She was in a daze. It seemed as if the car drove itself because Lisa sat oblivious of her surroundings. She could not stop the flow of tears. Lisa parked her car, got out, and staggered toward the formation. The tact Sergeants had already called the formation to attention as Lisa walked slowly toward them. Her uniform exhibited residue of her blood and soup. But she kept walking.

By the time she got to the formation to take her place in her squad, the Sergeant yelled, "FALL OUT!"

Soldiers stared at Lisa's appearance and began murmuring amongst themselves. Some were even laughing and stated 'Her boyfriend must have whipped her real good!' But Lisa just stood. She stood in hopes of the TACT Sergeants seeing her demise and having compassion. Everyone muddled around in hopes of gathering information about Lisa's dreadful appearance. Lisa continued to stand, still crying – still bleeding.

Soon one of the sergeants walked toward her running off the nosey, lingering peers. He asked, "What in the world happened, Clayton?"

Lisa said, with tears still streaming, "I was in a fight, Sergeant."

"I can see that much, but with who?"

Lisa's cries became audible, almost to the point of not controlling herself. The sergeant placed one hand on her shoulder, and she winced from the pain. He quickly removed it and asked,

"Clayton, who did this to you? You know you don't have to deal with this sort of treatment from anyone. I suggest you press charges."

Lisa sucked in a deep breath and with her deep inhale, mucus and tears joined forces causing her response to become muffled.

"I didn't quite understand you," the sergeant stated. He then leaned in closer to Lisa to hear her remarks and to provide a bit of privacy. "Please, repeat," said the Sergeant.

"My brother did this to me." After Lisa's reply, her legs became wobbly, and she was unable to stand. The Sergeant caught her before she went down and guided her to a place to sit.

He shook his head, and for a moment was at a loss for words. He hated to see Lisa in such despair for she was an outstanding soldier and would soon be recommended to lead the entire PLC UNIT as acting First Sergeant.

"Clayton," he said, "If you go to sick call, do you think you will be able to finish the course. You are allowed one visit to sick call."

Lisa looked up at the Sergeant with tears still streaming that intertwined with her bloody lip. She said, "I would love to finish, Sergeant." She put her head down and allowed the tears to drop freely, making a soft tapping sound on her pants leg. With her head down, she repeated, "I would love to finish."

CHAPTER XIX

"FALL IN!" shouted a strong, and confident Lisa Clayton. The soldiers followed her commands as she undoubtedly held the position of acting First Sergeant in PLC. A proud moment for Lisa, for she stood determined to follow her dreams. A prominent Lisa marched the PLC Unit up and down the quad. She passed out duties and inspected each one.

Meanwhile, Mason and Greg still lingered at the trailer, still not working. But Lisa no longer lived there. The TACT sergeant pressured her that it was time to move on – to move back into the barracks until they left the trailer. In addition, back at her primary duty station, the incident was reported to the First Sergeant, and he gave Lisa another room in the barracks, once she finished with PLC. Moving was sort of a challenge for Lisa, for she was afraid to go back to the trailer alone to get her things. Unbeknownst to her, the First Sergeant had arranged for some soldiers to help her retrieve her items after she graduated from the academy.

That day of graduation had finally come and Lisa graduated with honors. In just a few weeks she was due to appear before the E-5 board and put on another stripe. She stood so happy, in that she realized she had to be strong. Although it hurt her deeply that her brother would raise his hand to harm her, she found it in her heart to forgive. As far as living in that turmoil, she decided to follow her First Sergeant's advice and move out of the trailer.

Lisa, accompanied by four other soldiers pulled up to the trailer to get her belongings. She was not surprised to see Mason's car parked and parked in her parking spot. She swung open the door to the mobile home and found Greg and Mason chilling, watching TV. She looked back at the soldiers and said, "That TV is going, my stereo and all of the dishes."

The soldier who walked over to the TV, looked at Mason and Greg, and then at the TV, and he asked, "Are you talking about this TV?"

Lisa glanced back from the kitchen while packing dishes in a box and said, "Yep, that TV." She then stopped what she was doing and walked over to unplug it.

Greg gave her a stern look as if to say, 'You better not touch it!' But a strong Lisa accompanied by others outnumbered the woman abuser. She smiled while staring Greg right back into his eyes and 'SNATCHED,' went the sound of the cord coming from the wall.

Instantly, Greg rose to his feet. Mason also stood, and said, "Lisa, what are you doing?"

She answered, "What does it look like I'm doing? I am moving out! And guess what? You are too."

"But we don't have anywhere to go," Mason stated with his hands facing outward.

Lisa shot back, "That is not my problem! I refuse to take care of two grown tail men!"

She then walked past them and picked up a couple of throw pillows off the sofa. She whirled around and said, "I suggest you start beating the pavement and find someplace else to stay because I've told the landlord that I needed to get out of this lease."

Lisa then directed the soldiers to pick up the TV and take it to her car. Another one grabbed the stereo system, and she tossed the pillows to another. Mason grabbed his head in disbelief. He continued to try and persuade Lisa to change her mind. But she kept divvying out orders as to what will be taken out of the home. Greg rolled his eyes and began to walk toward the door. He stood just in front of Lisa and stared – she stared back and said silently, "Hit me if you want, and you won't live to see another day!"

It was as if Greg could feel what she was thinking because her eyes penetrated his so deeply, that he dropped his gaze and walked out the open door. Lisa didn't even walk to the door to see her brother leave, for she continued to instruct the soldiers what would be taken out of the trailer and what would stay. Mason finally looked around at the soldiers walking passed him, back and forth, gathering the items directed by Lisa. He soon walked over to the kitchen table, grabbed his keys, and stormed out the door. Soon the packing was complete, and Lisa and her entourage left for the barracks.

––––––––––

Lisa's life, to say the least, began to blossom. She continued to excel in her military status and like many other promises she had made to herself, she vowed to climb that ladder of success. As years continued to fleet by, things most important to her, began to change astronomically. She married a soldier and after vetting for what she thought to be a good catch soon deteriorated as he turned out to be a child abuser and tried his best to mentally abuse her. By now, Lisa had tuned into her spirituality and started worshiping the Lord as her mother had always instilled in her. Lisa served in the church at her last duty station, as an usher. She continued her education so she could have another occupation after she retired from the military. Lisa continued to follow every avenue that prompted advancement – even if it meant letting go of something she viewed as golden.

Upon her newfound journey in her spiritual life with Jesus, she thought that divorce was evil in God's sight. For she had read in the Bible that God hates divorce. She wanted so desperately to please God, and without discernment; she stayed in an abusive relationship longer than she should have. Her sons would complain how he, Gregory's stepdad, and Tim's biological father, would wait until she left for work and would beat them for the least little thing. These reports grew more frequent and finally, Lisa reported his actions to his Company Commander, where he withstood judicial punishment.

As Lisa grew spiritually, she began to delve into God's word more often and prayed for understanding. She discovered that yes, God our Father does hate divorce, but He has also called us to live in peace. She also found that the Lord said, "For I know the plans I have for you, plans to prosper, not to harm. Lisa prayed hard and asked God for guidance and He gave her an answer.

One morning she managed to muster up enough strength to file for a divorce. She needed peace of mind. And after 24 years of marriage, Lisa divorced a man whom she thought would be with her for eternity, at least on this side of Heaven. In this marriage, she suffered mental abuse – something she was not privy to. Mental abuse can be subtle in so many ways. One would have to be knowledgeable to be able to recognize its tyranny. As Lisa continued to delve into God's word, she discovered that a man is to love his wife as he loves himself. For a man will not cause harm to his own body.

———————————

Mental abuse can make you feel worthless, and no matter how hard you try to please the abuser, you *never* will. *You cannot change them*, but you can change your circumstances. You must share what you are going through with someone that you can trust such as a pastor, a praying partner, or a family member. Don't go at it alone, because you will lose. But if you are destined to survive, take some steps to motivate your decision to leave. It's okay – it is truly okay to leave an abuser. Choose your poison, either you stand up for yourself and leave on your own two feet or be carried by others.

———————————

After Lisa's divorce, she traveled home to visit her ailing grandmother.

"The hospice nurse said it won't be long now," said Laura. She then began to cry, because she felt as if Nancy did not have a fair shot at life. Laura thought back on the times Nancy constantly ran from her dad's stifling abuse. Laura really did not understand how she withstood it for so long. But, in Nancy's case, she had nowhere else to go. Paul was her sole provider. As Laura sat and pondered on Nancy's rough life, the hospice nurse walked out of Nancy's room and rendered a soft nod, gesturing for Laura and Lisa to come to say their goodbyes.

Upon entering her room, Laura and Lisa stood amazed that Nancy's eyes were open and she beckoned them to come closer. She whispered, "I'm going home now," Lisa sniffled. Nancy caught a glimpse of her grieving granddaughter, and she extended her weak trembling arm toward her. Lisa stepped closer to her grandmother and took her hand. Nancy managed to say with a raspy feeble voice, "It's okay my dear. I'm going to a place where no one can hurt me. There will be nothing but peace." Nancy then looked at her daughter and whispered, "Stay strong, be encouraged." A crying Laura nodded as tears flowed from her face.

Suddenly, Nancy tried to sit up, but she couldn't. She managed to point to her nightstand drawer. Her feeble body collapsed back onto her bed, she took in a deep breath and was gone.

"Grandma!" Lisa shouted. Laura took Lisa by the hand and led her out of the room.

The hospice nurse soon joined them. "Are you guys going to be okay until the funeral home comes?"

The grief-stricken women nodded. The hospice nurse nodded with a faint smile and left the home.

After Nancy's body was removed from the home, Laura and Lisa crept back into the bedroom where Nancy used to lay. They both sat on the bed and for a moment looked lost. Silence seared the air and neither knew what to do next. They had lost their rock. Laura thought, *what am I going to do now. Mama kept me grounded. She kept me safe from Perry.*

Lisa began to feel much guilt because she did not come home as she thought she should. She whispered to Laura, "I wished I would have come home more to visit."

Laura soothes, "Mama knew how busy you were."

Lisa then asked, "Do you think she knew all the mess I went through?"

"I believe so," Laura answered. "I only told her bits and pieces of what you shared with me."

"What did she say?" Lisa asked as she turned to face Laura.

"She said I'm going to pray that God delivers her."

After Laura's remark, she expressed a confused expression and said, "You know what? Now that I think about it after we would talk about some of the things you were going through, I would stop by her bedroom just to check on her. And as she recognized my presence, she would scramble to put something in her nightstand drawer." Laura paused for a second and placed a finger over her lip. She continued. "It was as if she was hiding something from me."

They sat – they pondered. It was as if a lightbulb went off at the same time. Both women jumped up from the bed and went to Nancy's nightstand. They stood and looked at each other as if they were about to impose on Nancy's privacy. But then they remembered her last motion before her death.

"She was trying to tell us something!" Laura spoke with excitement. Immediately, Lisa opened the top drawer, she scrambled, moving papers aside to see what, if anything, Nancy's last words would bring. Nothing was there. Laura stepped up, shaking her head from side to side saying, "No, it wasn't the top drawer, it was the bottom one." She then snatched it open and there lay a tattered notebook. Laura took it and she and Lisa sat on the bed thumbing through each page.

It seemed as if Nancy documented each day of her life. It was her personal diary. She wrote about the bad times as well as the good. There was one notation that really stood out to Laura and Lisa, and it read.

"A person sees no harm in ruining another's life. They hit, they spit and even sometimes kick. And the person on the receiving end tries to find solace, peace, and safety, no matter how small a space. You tried to make me feel small with your hateful words. Awe it doesn't matter, the closer the walls the safer I feel. I don't mind running to my place of refuge. It may be tiny, but that's all I have. It may not look good on the outside, but that's all I have. I feel comfortable here, I'm safe, and as long as I go to my safe place, you can't hit me anymore. Because no one wants to come to this place. It is a reminder, that they are seeking refuge.

"It is small, but I am safe. Maybe one day the tables will turn, and you will take on my habitation, but it won't be safe for you – naw, you can't feel comfortable in such a small place. Why? Because you

have embellished your stance to make me feel small. It will kill you to go where you've forced me. It's small but I'm safe. Why do you treat me so badly? Haven't I been loyal to you? Why do you see fit to minimize me? Nothing that I do seems to please you."

Lisa and Laura broke down at the words noted from Nancy's withering penmanship. As Laura closed the booklet, Lisa caught a glimpse of the front cover

. She shouted, "Mama, look!"

Laura quickly turned the book to the front cover; there she saw a faded title that read;

"DOGHOUSE." Laura sat, she thought about her mother's written words. She briefly rose.

Lisa noticed Laura's movement and asked, "Mama, where are you going?"

With a brief wave of her hand, Laura responded as she proceeded to walk out of the room, "I'll be right back."

Soon, Laura appeared with a diary of her own. She passed it to Lisa. Lisa looked at her mother as she received the diary. She opened it and as soon as she began to indulge in the notations, the tears flowed.

They both realized that Nancy, as far as they knew, was the first battered woman within their family. Next, it was Laura and now, Lisa. However, Nancy seemingly paved the way for them, and it was more than they could ever imagine, and by her diary, even though she had no permanent place to physically move to for protection, she did manage to stay out of reach of her abuser. The diary gave pertinent information on how Nancy knew when to retreat to her special place of safety. As they sat digesting Nancy's words of wisdom, they noticed more writings.

"This is almost too much for me to bear," Laura replied, after returning and picking up her mother's journal again.

"Me too, Mama," a tearful Lisa chimed.

"Let's take a break from these readings and start making some decisions for Mama's funeral," said Laura.

———————

The two women made funeral arrangements for Nancy. In the next few days, they found themselves getting dressed to attend. Laura just so happened to check in on Lisa after she got dressed.

"Lisa, are you about ready?"

"Yes, just let me get my jacket."

Lisa donned her military jacket and stepped out of the room. When Laura saw her, her eyes glazed with tears. Lisa said, "I hate that I am wearing my uniform now. I remembered you asked me to wear it with you to church when I first joined the military, but I didn't." Lisa looked down at it and remarked with a half-smile. "I'm surprised that I can still wear this thing."

Laura walked over to Lisa to console her, who by now was crying. "Oh, it's fine," Laura assured. "Besides, Mama got to see you in it from the pictures you sent home when you were in the Army." Laura looked up and stared off in the distance, "Ah, she loved to look at those pictures." She then looked at Lisa and said, "And you know she could tell if you had gained weight, lost weight, and what you were going through."

"Wow," Lisa responded.

Laura and Lisa left for Nancy's funeral. Afterward, they returned home to read more of Nancy's words of wisdom.

"Listen to this Mama," said Lisa.

'Laura, don't stand by and allow Perry to treat you like some animal. People hit animals to get them to do what they want them to do. Don't do that – no, you are better than that. Be strong. You make your own money. Save some just in case you have to flee."

Laura and Lisa discovered much more in that second drawer of Nancy's nightstand. For Nancy was a reader and she kept brochures on domestic violence.

As Laura perused the literature she said, "You know what? Mama used to tell me this stuff word for word, but I would not listen." She then looked at Lisa, "And I used to quote to you some of the same stuff."

Lisa interjected, "And I wouldn't listen."

They smiled, looked at each other, and said, "That's okay, we are now armed with a plethora of information. No more will a man raise his hand to me," spoke Laura. "And one better not raise his toward me," Lisa shot back, and she continued, "or, he will surely die."

Laura shook her head in disagreement and said, "No, no, there is no need for that. You won't be any better than he is if you kill him, Girl!" Laura smiled a big wide grin and said, "How about this, the next man who puts their hands on us, let's send them to the doghouse!"

Lisa nodded, "Yeah, I like that!" She then jokingly mimicked someone scolding a dog who had messed up, "Gone on, git! Go!" She stooped and shuffled her hands as if she were shooing an imaginary dog. "Go! Get on out of here!" The two laughed and made a vow, that this generation would never succumb to such violence again, no matter who tried to deliver it. They armed themselves with pertinent information and their vows soon came to fruition, because no other woman in that family fell prey to domestic violence again. Even down to Lisa's grandchildren, no not one.

———————————

There is an overabundance of information on protecting yourself during a domestic violence situation. Unlike women in the 1950s, women today are armed with viable information to allow them to survive domestic disputes and or abuse.

First off, let's choose to study a boyfriend's behavior before the relationship goes further. Watch for red flags before you get serious. Now, you may say, Terri, I'm not going around anxious about every man's behavior that I meet. I beg to differ. Do not step out of that lonely stage and settle because you are excited to be with someone. No, place that anxiety in focusing on his or her behavior. A person's behavior, within 30 days, will tell you a lot about them.

The Mayo Clinic's stance on domestic violence, also known as intimate partner violence, shares pertinent details on what to recognize from an abuser. I like to call them red flags.

The article notes:

1. **Name-calling and insults that put you down.**
2. **Tries to stop visits with family/friends, work, or seeking medical help**
3. **Tries to control where you go, how you spend money, what to wear**
4. **Threatens you with violence or a weapon**
5. **Physically hits, slaps, or kicks you.**
6. **Forces you to have sex against your will**
7. **Blames you for their behavior.**

These are just a few red flags, and remember, these instances are ongoing. There is a pattern. It is not a one-time thing.

The beauty of all of this madness is that there is hope; there is help. But you have to be willing to seek it. You do not deserve to be treated as such. Know your self-worth, and don't allow anyone to bring you down, ever.

There is a correlation between an abuser and their past. Learn a person's history.

In this book, the character Lisa is portrayed as me. Her first sight of physical violence was with her Dad. Secondly, with her first boyfriend, Tommy. He had a history. She did not see it until it was too late. What did his past foretell? He was recently divorced, which angered him. So, he took it out on Lisa. In this case, one would recognize her abuse as Intimate Partner Violence. Her notable red flag resulted in a violent strike. A man who hits you once will do it again.

Let's analyze Giles. He accrued an ugly history. But Lisa did not recognize it until it was too late. He possessed unfavorable conduct from the military. Something, Lisa stood unaware of. Lisa was new to the unit and a fast tracker. This meant she moved through the ranks fairly quickly. Her first encounter was a hit to her head. After the apology, another blow. In fact, he demonstrated all the above types of abuse. But Lisa ignored them and suffered unnecessary hardships because of it.

What about Mason? He came on the scene as a supporter, but he too had a history. Even though he appeared to be her protector, he too abused her. It wasn't mentioned in the storyline, but Mason bullied Lisa with a gun to the back of her head. It happened one morning while she got ready to go to work. An argument ensued. She tied her bootstraps, he intimidated her with his weapon. His history? He was released from the military.

So, arm yourself with information, no matter how adorable you think an individual may be. It is good to learn about their past and to know the signs. And remember, don't try to change a person because you can't.

If you find yourself in an abusive situation, immediately find a safe place to retreat to until you can leave safely. According to the Mayo Clinic, you should have a plan, a packed getaway bag with necessities, and hidden in a place that is easy to retrieve. Contact a close friend, one you can trust. Tell them what you're going through. Contact a spiritual leader from a local church; they can direct you to a women's shelter and help you find other safe places to go.

Don't stay in an abusive relationship because you feel there is no hope financially. Get your education. Open doors of opportunity to better support yourself.

Love yourself, and never allow others to put you down. God loves you. He has called you to live in peace. Don't give up! There is hope, and it lies within you.

INFORMATION ON DOMESTIC VIOLENCE/INTIMATE PARTNER VIOLENCE

VA U.S. Department of Veterans Affairs
INTIMATE PARTNER VIOLENCE
Intimate Partner Violence Safety Planning Guide
www.veteranscrisisline.net
1-800-273-8255 Press 1

MAYO CLINIC
Domestic Violence Against Women: Recognize Patterns, Seek Help
https://www.mayoclinic.org/healthy-lifestyle/adult-health/in-depth/
domestic-violence/art-20048397

WOMEN'S HEALTH ISSUES
Intimate Partner Violence and Safety Strategy Use: Frequency of Use and Perceived Effectiveness
www.whijournal.com

A SAFE PLACE
HOW TO BREAK UP
info@asafeplaceforhelp.org
24-Hour Crisis Line: (847) 249-4450 or 1-800-600-SAFE or TTY: 847-249-6557

SHADAE

IN LOVING MEMORY OF A BEAUTIFUL SOUL,
MY NIECE, SHADAE NICOLE ROSCOE

June 19, 1995 – May 3, 2022

Shadae stood determined to make a good life for herself and her son, Bryson. She attended nursing school and graduated with honors. Her dreams and tenacity catapulted her on a trajectory filled with non-stop success. I stood amazed at her willingness to give so much of herself to helping others.

Shadae recognized her gift from God. He instilled in her a giving heart. You can tell because she accomplished assigned tasks flawlessly. Many go throughout their entire life not recognizing their gift from the Lord, but not my niece. Doused with boldness, she stepped into divine responsibilities and delivered.

Her infectious smile drew you to her. Her delicate compassionate spirit soothed you. Concern for others became her aspiration and mission.

In such a short life, she accomplished more than others her age could only dream.

A tender sprout, she stood, a meaningful and caring heart she possessed, and a living passion giving her all so that others could be free of pain. That is who Shadae was, my beautiful niece and loving soul.

On May 3, 2022, she lost her life on this side of Heaven due to a senseless act of domestic violence. Even in death, she emits a legacy that will free and deliver others. That's Shadae, that's just how she lived.

BIOGRAPHY

Terri Britt Watts a native of Ahoskie, North Carolina, was born in January to the late Frank and Daisy Britt. Terri graduated from Ahoskie High School, now known as Hertford County High, in 1978. She left Ahoskie and joined the Army, where She served 20 years. Terri later retired from the Army on December 1, 2000, attended Fayetteville State University and earned a Bachelor's Degree in Psychology. She earned a Special Education Teacher License and taught Special Education for nine years. Terri attended graduate school and earned a Master's Degree in School Administration.

Terri finally fulfilled her lifelong dream of becoming an author. She published seven books, titled The Other Side Of My Prayers, Confronting The Guilt Of My Past, Your Body Is Your Temple, Bitter Root, Bitter Root II, Where Is Willie, and her most recent, DOGHOUSE. She shares an abundant life with her husband, David. Together they share four children and eight grandchildren. Terri's hobbies consist of reading her Bible, walking, biking, lifting light weights, mentoring teens, swimming, sewing, writing, cooking, traveling, and spending quality time with family and friends. Terri currently resides in Savannah, Georgia, with her husband, David.